KINGDOM OF THE SUN

KINGDOM OF THE SUN

Rise of a King

A. Gildersleeve

Library of Congress Control Number:		2012915907
ISBN:	Hardcover	978-1-4797-0821-5
	Softcover	978-1-4797-0820-8
	Ebook	978-1-4797-0822-2

This book was printed in the United States of America.

To order additional copies of this book, contact:
Xlibris Corporation
1-888-795-4274
www.Xlibris.com
Orders@Xlibris.com
111061

CONTENTS

CHAPTER ONE

A Tournament of Skills

THE WORLD OF Ainosia was at a turning point. Amid the serene hills, the thick forests, and even at the peaks of the dark mountains, there was tension thickening the air. People and creatures in every corner of the land had their mind's eye on the prosperous kingdom of Aranyhon. The law of Aranyhon dictated that the beloved Queen Aurora had to step down from the throne and name her successor. The kingdom was about to change.

"I would help you with your duties if you would take the throne," Aurora said to Sadah as they wandered through the castle's courtyard.

Sadah, a tall slender young woman with thick blonde curls, was Aurora's royal advisor and her dearest friend.

"I realize that," replied Sadah. "It is not the duties that concern me. It is the risks."

"What risks are you referring to exactly?"

Sadah looked grimly into Aurora's eyes. "You know your position is dangerous, Your Majesty. There are kingdoms surrounding us that are filled with villainy. If an attack was launched against us, who do you think they would look to capture and even kill?"

Aurora shrugged nonchalantly, but she knew of the dangers Sadah feared. Aranyhon was the largest kingdom in Ainosia, but the other kingdoms and regions surrounding it were quite treacherous. The outer regions of the map showed the lair of the vampires, but they had been incarcerated for nearly two decades now. Near their lair was slayer territory. The slayers were a people who fought against the vampires for centuries and now lived as a clan, hiding from the world in the deep caverns of the mountains. South of that territory was the land of the faeriefolk who were generally peaceful in nature. However, the faeries had a major conflict with the witches in the past. The war between the two societies resulted in the faeries forming an active army and the witches vanishing from the lands of Ainosia. No one knew where they lurked after the war. Further east from the faeriefolk was the Great Volcano of Galgamon. There was a dark magic there of which no one would speak. Warriors who went in search of the mountain's secrets never returned. Although these threats lay in the far stretches of the world they were all too close to Aranyhon.

The most imminent danger lay in the kingdoms of Morkslott to the east and Agorled to the north. These kingdoms bordered Aranyhon, which sat on the southeastern shoreline of the land. The other kingdoms kept Aranyhon cut off from the rest of the world. Their rulers had changed over the years but at this time the kingdoms were under the control of two usurpers. Agron, the monarch of Morkslott, was once a conniving, clever man. Morkslott was widely known for its military's muscle, and Agron had been their army's general when its previous king reigned. He was the king's confidant, his advisor, and, supposedly, his friend. Then the king suddenly fell ill and strangely decreed that Agron was to be his heir, even though his eldest son had birthright. It was then that the people of Morkslott grew distrustful of Agron. All the while, Agron maintained he had no hand in the king's sad demise and, furthermore, that he never had desired the throne for himself. Prince Arauck, the true heir to Morkslott's throne, led his people in rebellion, and Agron became desperate to subdue them. Rochero, a notorious witch, came to Agron's aid. With his command of magical forces, Rochero was able to quash the rebellion and stabilize Morkslott for Agron. For his efforts, Agron granted Rochero a place in his court as his royal advisor and court sorcerer. Once this alliance was made, the people of Morkslott became even more frightened of Agron. After Prince Arauck disappeared into hiding, they were left with no choice but to submit. The longer he and Rochero were in power, the more erratic Agron's behavior became. Where he had once been a strategic genius and capable soldier, Agron had become skittish and thoroughly unstable. Despite his paranoia he became addicted to power and was determined to keep Morkslott for his own. Therein lay the danger. Agron's lust for power could only lead to trouble.

Then there was Jedah, the sorceress queen of Agorled. Agorled had once been a thriving kingdom. At that time, its lands were filled with lush countryside much like Aranyhon. But once Jedah gained control, it turned into a wasteland. Where once its fields had smelled of sweet grass and dandelions, now Agorled reeked of rotting wood and ash. The forest that surrounded the dark crumbling castle was dry and barren. Jedah had no human subjects, but there were rumors that she had other followers. As far back as the history of Ainosia was written, Jedah had been a part of it. Yet she bore no signs of advanced age. Her name plagues the pages of the ancient texts, even before the war between faeries and witches occurred. She was said to have caused the war itself, but no one ever told the tale of how. Jedah was also widely known for her alliance with the vampire overlord Jaqtra until the vampires were cursed into captivity. No one knew who had been Jedah's tutor, but the magic that Jedah practiced was as dark as her kingdom. She had stolen the throne from Agorled's previous ruler only fifteen years before this time, and she seemed content to rule over Agorled for the time being.

Jedah knew little of Aurora, but Aurora knew all too well the horrifying deeds Jedah had done. Aurora had tried, for the entirety of her term, not to think too much of Jedah's control over Agorled. But it haunted her that Jedah appeared to be waiting for something. As much as it pained her to admit it, Aurora knew that Sadah was right in believing there were real threats in Ainosia.

"I suppose I can respect your disinterest in the throne," Aurora said to Sadah. "Being queen is a dangerous position. I may even be at risk once I name a successor. I think once I step down I should have some spells cast over me to change my appearance. I think mahogany-colored hair and green eyes would disguise me well enough, don't you think?"

Sadah shook her head and laughed in response to the joke. "No, Your Majesty, I think your dusty blonde hair and blue eyes can remain, but perhaps we can find you some tattered clothes and maybe a pig farm for a home."

Aurora tried to look insulted but could only laugh.

"All right, if we are to get me to my pig farm, we had better find a means of choosing a proper successor. I must have an opportunity to truly know the person I am to pass the crown to, seeing as how there is no one I know personally who is interested." She shot Sadah one last hopeful glance.

"It's true, it has been decades since a ruler was unable to find a member of their court to succeed them," Sadah said shooting a resolute look back at the queen. "Therefore, you will need to determine and analyze the strengths and weaknesses of all those who do wish to be in power."

"I would say that I could conduct interviews, but how many applicants would we have? And how am I to know what their true intentions behind ruling are? It would be far too easy for someone to take power that should not. We need something more challenging."

"Perhaps a tournament could be held to test the personal skills of the candidates? Skills that only a certain someone can assess properly?" suggested Sadah with a bemused grin.

"Yes," said Aurora, "someone like our friend in the tall tower. Brilliant, Sadah! A tournament will allow the entire kingdom to be part of the proceedings, while still making the throne a bit of a challenge to claim."

"If I may say so, Your Majesty, Agron and Jedah will try to intercept the crown."

"I agree and the laws of succession only state that to take the throne, an individual must be at least sixteen years of age. Therefore, I shall set in place a restriction to disqualify Agron and Jedah from the trials. Only those that are true to Aranyhon may enter the tournament."

Sadah's eyes narrowed. "Isn't that a bit vague?"

Aurora smiled. "I think it will serve the purpose. Again, we will rely on our friend in the tower to work out the details."

Aurora's announcement sent a surge of excitement throughout the kingdom. Many older men and women wished their children to attempt the challenges. A few takers would show themselves in due time. As the word was spread by traders and other townspeople who traveled beyond the safety of Aranyhon, knowledge of the tournament reached Agron's castle.

"There must be a way!" boomed Agron. "She can't just shut out a person like that! It's not right! I make an excellent king!"

"Of course you do, my lord," said Rochero, Agron's court sorcerer who faithfully stood by. Agron flopped down on his throne, biting his nails.

"They think I can't handle it," Agron said, pointing out the window toward the courtyard of his castle. "They think I've lost my mind! Aurora doesn't know anything about that. Why would she not let me compete for Aranyhon's crown? It's not fair, I tell you!"

"If my lord would permit me to speak," said Rochero.

Agron dashed to the table that Rochero sat at, looking hopefully into Rochero's dark sunken eyes.

"My lord is not considering the powers I have at my disposal," said Rochero. "I can easily gain you access into the tournament through means of a disguise. You only need tell me who you wish to appear as—perhaps someone of some notoriety in Aranyhon so that no one would suspect villainy."

Agron's eyes widened, but his muscles relaxed.

"Of course," he said, "someone of notoriety. But it has to be someone just thick enough to believe I mean no harm to Aranyhon. Otherwise, how will we lure him here for the spell casting?"

"Genius, my lord," said Rochero, the corner of his mouth curling in pleasure.

Agron grinned. "Yes, I think I can find someone. You are sure that you can overcome the obstacles put in place by Aurora?"

Rochero beamed, "Have I ever led you astray, my lord?"

Meanwhile, far from Agron's castle lay the kingdom of Agorled and its ruler, who also had heard of Aranyhon's coming vulnerability. And there Jedah sat, high upon her throne. Cloaked by a heavy black cape, she appeared to be a hole of darkness. Her eyes were black; her skin was bloodless and seemed pasty in contrast to her black velvet gown. Beneath the hood of the cloak, her fiery red hair was piled high on her head in a mass of ringlets. The warm orange flame of the fire roaring in the middle of the large hall was the only light around the walls of dark gray stone. Vines that were vastly overgrown, entering through the window, crawled all over the room. Jedah paid the castle no mind as it rotted beneath her feet. The fire gave off immense heat, and yet the room still was chilly. A freezing air seemed to be pouring from the woman seated on the throne.

A man sat on a small wooden stool to Jedah's left. The stool was so low to the ground that the man's bony knees were pulled up to his chest, nearly touching his chin. He looked like a mere skeleton with just the thinnest layer of dry and cracked skin pulled taut over his bones. He could have fallen dead at any moment, but once Jedah began to speak, he was revived and hung on her every word.

"I will take Aranyhon from Aurora," she growled. "That mockery of a queen will fall before me. Once Aranyhon has fallen, Morkslott will follow easily, and I will finally have attained the power I rightly deserve."

"My lady," the small man squeaked, "Queen Aurora is a strong ruler, and many love her. How do you plan to defeat her?"

Jedah chuckled. "My dear Phober, Aurora may be popular, but she has no mind for ruling a kingdom. Her soul is weak, and she knows little of the ways of the world. Aurora concerns herself with her friends and with her people. She is no match for me. I—a sorceress who has gained magical powers, with the strength to raise creatures from the dead, to conjure fire from the very earth, and to divine the nature of the future—I have spared her thus far only in the hopes that she would present me with an opportunity to claim her lands for my own. Now is that time, and her popularity will not save her when I attack swiftly and without warning."

"What will you do, my lady?"

Her mouth broke into a small grin. "I will wait and allow my eyes and ears to do their work."

A sneer crossed her face as she looked to her right at a box sitting on a table. She opened the lid, and Phober let out a small gasp. An army of black spiders scrambled out of the box to the floor. One crawled onto Phober's arm, and he tried not to shudder as it glared at him with its numerous, black eyes.

"Bring me the information I need, my loves," ordered Jedah, and the spiders began to scamper out of the dark room and head for the Aranyhon border.

The next day, Aurora and Sadah woke early to begin preparations for the tournament. There was only one person they could rely on to create a tournament fit for choosing a worthy sovereign for Aranyhon. They walked to the far north corner of the castle and began to climb the tallest tower, one hundred and three steep steps in all. As they reached the door at the top, Aurora and Sadah fell with exhaustion into the room. A strong scent of incense gave vigor to their weary bodies, and they began to rise from their knees. The room was cluttered with books. The walls bore paintings of the far-off territories of Ainosia, mighty griffins, and colorful sunsets. A slender woman stood on the far side of the room.

"Your Majesty!" she said as she whirled around, her purple cloak knocking over a globe, which she just barely caught. "What a pleasant surprise! Will you have some tea? You too, Lady Sadah! Come! Come!"

She gestured for Aurora and Sadah to sit at a small table in the middle of the room—the only piece of furniture not covered with papers or books—as she pranced over to the fireplace to fetch hot water. Aurora and Sadah sat down and grinned at each other. The woman dancing around the room, busy as a bee, was known as Veradella. She was no older than Sadah or Aurora; in fact, all three were just nearing thirty years. But even as young as she was, Veradella's hair was a shiny silver color. It always had been. Her eyes were hazel and filled with all the joyful zeal you'd find in a child, yet all the depth and history of an elderly woman. Her gentleness was overwhelming, and it was difficult to imagine just how much power she held. Veradella was a witch—a slightly eccentric witch. But her childlike personality never had hindered her in a dire situation. She was too wise and skillful to allow it. There was no one more fluent in the history of magic in Aranyhon than Veradella, but she would never boast of her knowledge or abilities.

Veradella tiptoed back to the table with the hot water, slightly burning her fingers as she put the kettle down. The three sat and chatted for a while. Aurora had not seen Veradella recently because Veradella so rarely left the confines of her tower. She was always studying and learning something new, and very often, Aurora would find that Veradella's powers had vastly expanded the next time they met. Finally, the time came for Aurora to tell Veradella the news about the tournament. Veradella's face lit with excitement as Aurora and Sadah explained their idea.

"A tournament? A celebration?" squeaked Veradella. "Oh, Your Majesty, I can hardly wait!"

"We will, of course, need your assistance," added Sadah, "in preparing the challenges."

"Yes," said Aurora, "we need the challenges to truly examine the contenders' personalities. So we need someone who has, shall we say, a creative mind to create them accordingly."

"Someone who is, perhaps, a little peculiar?" said Veradella, proudly. "Someone like me! I will be glad to help with what I can. When do we start?"

"Immediately! We have little time to waste," answered Aurora. "I would like you to start preparing the challenges today. This tournament should commence as soon as possible so as to not draw too much attention from outsiders."

The two exchanged looks, and Veradella understood.

"My time is at your disposal," chimed Veradella, "but might I ask a favor of you, Your Majesty?"

"Anything," said Aurora.

"Well," began Veradella, "I have an apprentice at the moment that has been staying on my sofa." Veradella gestured to a tattered piece of furniture that had feathers spilling out of a tear in one of its cushions. "And I would rather develop these challenges in complete seclusion. Would it be possible for him to remain in the castle until after the tournament?"

"I don't see why that would be a problem." Aurora smiled.

Sadah, who was a bit more cautious than Aurora, spoke up, "Who is this young man, Veradella?"

"Oh, his name is Amon," Veradella replied. "He's a fine young man, very sweet and very smart. I imagine his magical skills will surpass mine one day once he has been fully trained."

"So there is much talent in him then. Where did you find him?" asked Sadah.

Veradella's face went a tad gray, and her eyes seemed to stop shining. Aurora saw the sudden change and took concern. Veradella was very talented but could be naïve at times.

"Veradella," Aurora said, "where is Amon from?"

"Don't be angry, Your Majesty," she began. "He's such a bright, happy boy."

"Veradella." went Sadah in a firm tone.

Veradella's eyes shot away from Sadah and Aurora and to the wall. "I met Amon near the border of Agorled."

Aurora took a deep breath in and let out a stern sigh. It was dangerous to bring someone from Agorled to Aranyhon. Jedah did not keep human subjects, so the presence of a human in Agorled could mean nothing but trouble.

"Veradella," scolded Sadah, "you know that we cannot completely trust creatures from there! He could be a spy or an assassin! And if he has such strong powers, which I'm sure Jedah is aware of, who knows what damage he could do! I am very—"

"Sadah, please, I'm sure Veradella has good reason for bringing Amon here. Although I may not trust him, I will allow him to stay in my castle, under close watch of course," Aurora spoke in a firm tone.

Sadah's mouth dropped. "But," she began and then whispered, "Aurora."

"My decision is final," Aurora said gently. "Veradella, bring the young man to the throne room when he returns. Where is he now?"

"I sent him to the marketplace to get me some things," she replied. "He should be back soon."

"Until then, Veradella," said Aurora, "we shall be down in the throne room."

"Thank you for your patience and understanding, Your Majesty," said Veradella, the color returning to her face.

Aurora and Sadah began to make their way down the long staircase.

"Aurora—Your Majesty, what are you thinking?" said Sadah. "How can you possibly allow this boy to stay here? He's a threat to you and the kingdom!"

"Sadah, calm yourself," said Aurora gently. "I'll have Marvino keep an eye on him."

Aurora proceeded, but Sadah paused in her tracks. "Marvino? That does not make me feel any better."

Aurora smirked back at Sadah as they rounded a corner of the stairs. Just as she looked back, she felt herself collide with someone, and Aurora fell back onto Sadah. Just as they landed, both saw a scrawny boy tumbling away from them down the stairs to a landing. The young man had dark hair and eyes and was gangly, as if he had been stretched too tall. He wore a tattered shirt and pants that were patched everywhere. A basket of vegetables, fruit, and a loaf of bread were all over the staircase and landing. The boy was as startled as Aurora and Sadah. He began to scramble about to collect the items and place them back in the basket.

"I am so sorry!" said the boy.

Aurora picked herself up and helped Sadah up too. "It's all right, lad," she said, smiling at the boy who had not even looked up from the vegetables yet. "You must be Amon."

"You're Queen Aurora!" He gasped as he looked up. As his jaw dropped, he dropped everything he was holding too and bowed his head. "Your Majesty! I'm so very sorry!"

"You already said that," Aurora said. "You must be rushing up to deliver these items to Veradella. Run along for now. She will be bringing you to see me."

Amon's face went white. He swallowed hard as he went back to picking up the food.

Aurora nodded and rounded the corner. "See you shortly, Amon."

Sadah looked Amon up and down carefully as she followed Aurora.

"My lady," Amon said to Sadah, "mind the—"

Sadah felt her shoe sink deeply into something soft and a burst of juice sprayed her ankle and foot.

"—tomato," he said as he squeezed his eyes shut.

Sadah's left shoe was covered in tomato juice and the remains of the tomato stuck to her heel. She looked at Amon sternly but realized it really wasn't his fault. She removed the tomato, and Amon handed her a hankie to wipe her hand with. Aurora, who had witnessed the whole incident, held back a laugh but could not keep herself from grinning. She and Sadah then returned to the throne room, with Sadah muttering the entire way about how she'd never be able to get the tomato stains out of her dress.

Amon finally gathered up all the food and made his way up to Veradella's. As he entered the room, he saw Veradella staring out her window.

"Lady Veradella? I've returned with your things," he said. "I'm afraid some of the apples might be bruised. You see I . . . dropped the basket."

"It'll be fine, Amon, thank you," she replied but continued to stare out her window.

Amon emptied the items from the basket and put them away. He kept very quiet as it seemed that Veradella was concentrating. Once he finished, he moved to Veradella's side. Her face, he saw, was as stern as he'd ever seen it and was lined with concern.

"My lady?" he began. "Is everything all right?"

"I'm afraid not," she said. "Look."

She pointed out the window to a black cloud in the sky. It was to Aranyhon's north, over Agorled. Amon felt a chill go down his spine.

"Lady Jedah must be angry about something," said Veradella, watching Amon's expression very carefully. Amon froze. He could feel her gaze hitting his cheek. "What do you suppose it could be?" she asked.

He didn't look at Veradella at all. After a long pause, he said, "Perhaps she's lost something very important to her."

His voice was broken, and his answer sounded final. Veradella could sense he was nervous, and she didn't wish to push him any further. They stood in silence and watched the black cloud spin and grow over the kingdom to the north.

"You lost him?"

The hall shook as Jedah's voice echoed throughout.

"What do you mean you lost him? He's only a boy!"

"A very powerful boy, my lady," whimpered Phober. "He must have used some kind of spell to release himself from the dungeon!"

"He's just a boy without any training! He can't even control the craft yet! What you're trying to tell me is that you failed me—you and your idiotic guards! And I now hold *you* personally responsible!"

She was now standing, towering over Phober who was curled in a ball, cowering on the floor.

"M-m-my la-a-dy, I am so sorry, please."

"Don't plead with me," she growled. "You know you deserve this!"

"Of course, my lady! I do not deserve your mercy, but . . . please don't!"

Jedah's eyes were crazed and seemed to grow red with anger. She raised her hand as if to strike Phober. But rather than striking him, a ball of fire formed in her hand. Phober threw himself backward, preparing himself for death. He curled up and tried to cover his head with his skinny arms. But just as her ball of fire had grown to the size of a human skull, Jedah's eyes returned to normal, and she began to lower her hand. She extinguished the fireball, and she sank begrudgingly back into her throne.

"You're not worth my magic," she growled. "I have to save my strength for someone else."

Phober who was covered in sweat squeaked, "Wh-wh-ooo, my lady? Queen Aurora?"

Jedah rolled her eyes. "No, you fool! If you aren't worth my simplest magic, Aurora certainly isn't. But there is a young start-up that needs to be taught a lesson."

Amon walked silently behind Veradella down the long corridor to the throne room. The hall glistened under the bright sunshine that shot in through the large windows. He saw the tall doors of the throne room open. Veradella quickened her steps, and they passed through into the grandest room Amon had ever seen. The floor was emerald marble, the ceiling was pure white with an intricate pattern carved into it, and the walls were lined with mirrors reflecting the magnificence of the room over and over. At the far end sat Aurora on a throne of white marble with soft velvet cushions that matched the floor. Two large emeralds were encased in the armrests of the throne. They were so polished that Amon could see his reflection in them. Just above the headrest of the throne was a golden sun slightly raised off the marble. Amon had seen suns like this before at the metal worker's shop in the village, and he assumed this sun was Aurora's royal insignia. This sun was metal worked onto every shield that every guard carried, as well as embroidered on every banner he had seen hanging within the confines of the kingdom. The sun had the same tone of gold as Aurora's hair and glistened with the same luster. Within the sun's core was a second circle, and through the entire core was drawn a vertical line dividing the center of the sun. Amon felt sure that the shapes created by the line meant something, but his eyes had been drawn from them to the vast rays that protruded out from the core. These rays were masterfully curved and evenly spaced, giving them the appearance of the helm of a ship. Amon felt sure if he could touch them, he could set the sun spinning much like its celestial counterpart. When his eyes finally shifted from the magnificent golden sun, Amon noticed that Aurora was looking at him with an expression of amusement. Sadah, who sat next to Aurora on a smaller white marble seat, looked less than comfortable with his presence and glared in his direction, as if she could see directly into his heart. Amon felt himself shudder under her gaze. Veradella halted a few feet in front of the throne and made a low curtsy. Amon bowed low and when he stood up, he kept his eyes down.

"Your Majesty," Veradella began, "May I present Amon, my apprentice."

"Thank you, Veradella. Amon, come forward, please," replied Aurora.

Amon, his eyes still lowered, walked forward to meet Aurora who had risen from her throne to meet him.

"Are you afraid that you will turn to stone should you look at me, Amon? Never be afraid to look someone in the eye. No one's soul is superior to anyone else's," Aurora said. Amon looked up and into Aurora's eyes. She began to speak again, "Now I understand that Veradella found you on the border of Agorled." Amon's heart quickened, and his eyes hit the floor again. Aurora tried to keep her voice kind but firm. "Amon, I just want to know your intentions behind training in witchcraft?"

"Your Majesty," Amon began, "I never even knew I had powers until I met Lady Veradella. It's true she found me on Agorled's border, but I promise you, I am no Agorledian."

"Then what are you?" asked Sadah.

Amon was at a loss for words, and his brow and neck began to perspire. He didn't know what he could tell the Queen. His past, his present, he wasn't sure about any of it. Aurora looked calmly into his eyes. She could see no streak of evil in him. If this boy was a threat, he was a threat that was beyond Aurora's ability to detect. Aurora spoke but kept her eyes on Amon, "He has already told us, Sadah, he is no Agorledian. You may go, Amon, Marvino will be waiting for you outside, and he shall show you to your quarters."

Sadah sighed nervously as she looked in disbelief at Aurora.

Once in the hall, Veradella abruptly turned to Amon.

"You have been granted clemency. My advice to you is to not give Queen Aurora any reason to distrust you."

"My lady, why would I do anything to offend Queen Aurora?"

Veradella looked intently at Amon, but then her face suddenly fell as her eyes drifted beyond Amon out the window. The skies to the west were now growing dark. Veradella moved past Amon and studied the sky. After a moment she turned around swiftly.

"Amon, wait here for Marvino," she said. "I must speak with the queen again. Remember what I said."

Amon nodded and Veradella disappeared into the throne room once more. He was alone and he felt a shiver come over him as he looked at the other dark sky in the west.

In the castle of Morkslott, Rochero stood before his cauldron mixing a powerful elixir, one that would help Agron penetrate the borders of Aranyhon and enter the contest for the crown.

"It'll never work," said Agron, pacing nervously. "Veradella will have thought of such an obvious trick. How will this disguise deceive her?"

"Not to worry, Master. Veradella is powerful, but I know of no such charm that will allow her to look into your heart and see you for who you truly are. This potion can change you into another person for a day. You said you had a person to use?"

"Yes," Agron squeaked, "I have fooled that idiot guard of Aurora's into believing that I merely would like to be a spectator at the tournament. He will be here tomorrow to meet with me."

He let out a small laugh but quickly covered his mouth. "We must keep this quiet, Rochero," he said. "The people cannot know our plans." Agron ran to the window and pulled the drapes shut. "They think I'm no good, Rochero. They think I'm insane. I'm not insane, am I, Rochero?"

"Of course not, my lord," said Rochero, adding one last bottle of greenish liquid to the cauldron. "Now write down the name of the man and add the paper to the mixture. Then you and I can spend the day of the tournament in Aranyhon undetected!"

"Oh, thank goodness, I was hoping you'd come. You know I get nervous outside the castle on my own."

"I know, my lord."

"How will you enter Aranyhon?"

"I made myself a basic potion to change my appearance to that of a townsman of Aranyhon. Not to worry. No one will recognize me."

Agron smiled and took out a piece of paper and wrote down the name.

Marvino

He tossed it into the bubbling sea of green. They watched quietly as it dissolved in the potion.

Crash! The sound of a vase shattering echoed down the hall and practically scared Amon out of his skin. Suddenly, a figure could be seen stumbling around the corner and down the hall toward him.

"Hello there!" called the figure. "You must be Amon!"

"Uh . . . yes, yes I am," answered Amon trying to make out a face on the figure.

"Well, I'm Marvino," he replied, as he stepped into the light of the large windows. He had a large, warm smile and Amon thought he did have the look of a guard at all, but rather that of an overgrown playmate for a small child. His eyes sparkled and his demeanor was something like a funny, skittish forest creature.

"Well," said Marvino, "shall we get you settled in, then?"

Amon nodded.

"Well, all right then. Don't you have any things?"

"No," said Amon quickly, "I didn't think I'd be staying here long."

"Oh, well I'll speak to Queen Aurora. I'm sure we can get you some more personal items than what you're wearing!"

"Oh no, that won't be necessary. I'm perfectly happy with what I have."

"Nonsense, I'm sure her Majesty will be happy to lend a hand."

Amon saw he'd never win this battle, so he just smiled. Marvino led him through a series of halls, staircases, and doors. The palace was gorgeous from floor to ceiling. There was a great deal of sunshine coming through the enormous windows that made the rooms radiant. On the southern side of the castle, Amon could see the waves of the ocean rushing up to meet the shore. The millions of sparkles dumbfounded him. Each picture frame, doorway arch, table, and chair in those halls was accented in brass or gold. They came to a door across the way from one of the hundreds of large windows overlooking the village, and Amon suddenly realized he had no idea how they had arrived there. Marvino opened the door to the chambers, and Amon beheld a room decorated in deep blue. The bed was huge, with a diamond-patterned canopy over it and silver trim on all of its linens. There were three windows that had a bench seat and a door at the far side of the room, which led to a bath and dressing area.

"Well, here you are! You remember how to get here then?" asked Marvino.

"Yes, I think so," lied Amon.

"All right then. I'll leave you to get settled and comfortable," Marvino grinned and turned to leave, knocking into a vase of flowers. *Whoosh!* Just as they began to fall, Amon threw his hands up quickly to catch them, and the vase and flowers hung in midair. They did not waver, but held their position as solid as rock.

Amon's eyes widened. "I did it!"

"You certainly did!" exclaimed Marvino. "That's a pretty good trick! Wish I could do that. It would save Lady Veradella a good deal of time that she spends cleaning up after my clumsiness."

They laughed. Amon placed the vase back on the table, and Marvino took his leave. Once he was alone, Amon stretched out on the enormous soft bed. He had done it—his first piece of real magic, without any help from Veradella. He couldn't wait to tell her. She'd be so proud. The bed was so soft unlike Veradella's featherless sofa, and Amon began to realize how tired he felt. As he replayed his moment of magic over and over in his mind, he drifted off to sleep.

CHAPTER TWO

The Presence of Conflict

"YOUR MAJESTY, I don't think it is anything to concern ourselves with at the present moment, but it is worrisome that there are dark clouds spreading from both of our adversaries at the same time," Veradella said calmly.

"But we have no idea how soon they might strike, although I'm sure we have till the tournament. That would be the most obvious time they would both choose to attack," Aurora said as she paced calmly.

"Agron and Jedah would never join forces, Your Majesty. They could not stand each other long enough, no, not even to attempt to destroy you," Sadah remained seated, but she was rigid.

"I have no doubt that the two would never join forces against me, but that does not remove the threat of them attacking at the same time. All of Ainosia must know that my term as sovereign is coming to a close, and it does make Aranyhon vulnerable. It would be so simple for someone to swoop in and steal the throne now. Veradella, I want you to be sure that it is impossible for anyone that is not a true Aranyhoner to enter this tournament. I will not risk having Agron deceive us all. The cloud spreading from Morsklott surely indicates he has Rochero weaving spells already. As for Jedah, I highly doubt she will even care about the tournament. She will only use it to cover her usurpation. Therefore, our only choice is to be on our guard." With these words, Aurora returned to her throne. Her face was flushed, and her eyes shifted, showing that her mind was working quickly, but efficiently.

Sadah and Veradella exchanged looks of uncertainty.

Veradella spoke carefully, "Your Majesty, but what of your—"

"Silence!" Aurora snapped as she jumped to her feet. As she did so, her glass of wine on the table next to her hit the floor and shattered. All of their eyes shot to the glass. Aurora froze, and Sadah and Veradella exchanged looks again.

"It's nothing," Aurora said calmly, "and I am sorry for my curtness, but Veradella we must never speak of that. Not as long as I am queen. I thank you for making me aware of the threat that is upon us. As my two dearest friends, you know me better than anyone. This means that you know why I must remain as I am at this time."

"Yes, Your Majesty," Sadah replied and Veradella nodded.

Aurora's eyes drifted to the shattered glass. Slowly the shards of glass came together to form a glass again and returned itself to the table. Aurora smiled and looked to Veradella. "Thank you, Veradella, and now I think that will be all for today. Sadah please leave me for a while. Perhaps you could go inform Amon that dinner will be served shortly."

Veradella and Sadah left the throne room; they knew that Aurora would need some time.

"She must know that it is getting more and more dangerous to keep this façade up," Veradella whispered to Sadah as they shut the doors of the throne room. "She can't possibly think this tournament will go on without any trouble."

"I don't think that she intends for it to go on without trouble, Veradella. I think she may want to end this feud once and for all." Sadah kept her eyes straight ahead as she walked.

"But at the expense of the people? Sadah, you can't expect me to believe that she has given up on peace."

"She hasn't given up on peace . . . she just realized the presence of conflict. I think her decision is a good one. She can't hide from her fate forever."

Veradella's voice became firm, "If Agron or Jedah come to Aranyhon, our people will suffer. What will happen should they both arrive on the same day?"

"Calm down, Veradella." Sadah turned to face her friend. "Aurora is not crazy, nor is she rash. I'm sure she knows the consequences this event could have, but there must be a reason that she has chosen to take the risk. She's our friend. We must trust her."

Veradella let out a small sigh. "Sadah, you don't think she might be acting out of weariness do you? She's had to fight this fight for so long. I just don't know if she has the strength in her to hold on and still manage to protect her kingdom. She's fighting terrible inner demons and I don't want to see her suffer anymore . . . I shan't be at dinner. There is much to do."

Veradella began to leave, and Sadah turned away to look at the dark clouds creeping closer to Aranyhon. "We're her friends, Veradella. Whatever she decides to do, we protect her at all cost."

Veradella and Sadah's eyes met and Veradella nodded.

After a practically silent dinner with Sadah and Amon, Aurora went to her chambers for an early night. Her chambers were stashed away in the southern wing where the castle did not share borders with Morkslott or Agorled. Her room was burgundy and gold, with a balcony looking out across the ocean. The rhythm of the waves on the shore was relaxing, and the sky to the south was filled with stars—at least she could not see the impending clouds of Agron and Jedah. But truth is not always visible, and Aurora was sick with worry. She knew that her two enemies would take every opportunity to supplant her. With these thoughts weighing on her, she got ready for bed. As soon as her head fell onto the soft pillows, she was asleep. Her mind was filled with visions of a green countryside, with flowers covering the fields. A light breeze whistled through the air and swept softly against her cheeks. Then a small girl with golden hair came over the hillside. The girl had a gentle smile and let out a sweet laugh as she ran down a hill, the grass almost as tall as she. She turned toward Aurora, and Aurora realized that she was seeing her six-year-old self. She watched as her younger self turned from her and looked to the sky. Just then the sky grew dark, and light rain started to fall. Her younger self turned to Aurora and *flash!* A bolt of lightning crashed, and there was a dark figure standing on the hill behind her young self. Aurora awakened with a start. The sun was not yet up, but the first signs of daylight were peaking over the horizon. She went to her dressing room to prepare for the day. She wouldn't tell them, they did not need to know about her dream. It wasn't important.

Amon woke up early that day to find Veradella. He still had not seen her since he succeeded in freezing the vase, and he was dying to tell her. He made his way toward her tower, getting lost a little on the way. When he finally reached it, he raced up the stairs. After catching his breath, he knocked calmly and politely on the door.

"My lady, it's Amon," he called. "I know that you're busy but I really must tell you something . . . something that I was able to do."

He heard some shuffling in the room, and then the door clicked open. He entered as Veradella was putting one last book away in a drawer and she continued to shuffle papers as they spoke.

"Amon, how are you?" asked Veradella. "Hope the room in the castle is comfortable."

"Oh yes, my lady, it's wonderful—"

"And I hope you had a fine dinner last night, so sorry I had to miss it."

"Oh yes it was delicious, but I really must tell you—"

"Now, my dear, I am busy so I really must ask you to run along."

"But, my lady, I did some magic!"

Veradella stopped. "Magic? You did? Alone? And unassisted?"

"Yes," piped Amon, "I froze a vase in place. It was about to fall off a table and I stopped it in midair!"

"Was anyone with you?" asked Veradella, stepping closer to Amon.

He was surprised by Veradella's concerned expression, "Yes, that guard Marvino was with me at the time."

"Marvino . . ." Veradella slowly began to pace, "and did he stop moving as well?"

"No. Only the vase froze in place."

"Good gracious. Sounds like you have a bit of control over your power, Amon," she feigned a smile but still looked concerned and continued to pace.

"Control, my lady?"

Veradella stopped. "Yes, Amon, control." Her smile was genuine, and her tone was light again. "You see, every witch has a Nexus, a certain specialized power. We refer to them as our Nexus because our special power is at the center of our being. We are bound to our Nexus and it to us. We cannot alter it just as we cannot alter the nature of our hearts."

"Why would a person want to part with their Nexus?" asked Amon.

Veradella hesitated, "There are some powers a person would never wish upon themselves, Amon. Magic can come at a great cost to a witch. I know one person, in particular, who would give anything to change the gift been granted to them."

"What is my Nexus, exactly?" he asked.

"Your Nexus is chronoseizure, which is the ability to freeze objects in motion. Most likely you will be able to manipulate time as your power develops further. It's a unique power, one that I have never seen present itself as a Nexus. Now when a witch begins to learn chronoseizure, usually they will stop an entire room in its tracks, until they learn to control it and be able to fixate their magic only on the object that needs freezing. Do you understand? It usually takes a few years to master such a talent but you have managed to develop control instinctually. It's very . . . impressive."

Amon smiled at this. He had hoped Veradella would be proud.

"But," she began again, "it also is troublesome to me that one so young should have such power."

His heart sank.

Veradella spoke gently but firmly now, "Amon, some witches can use their magic in such evil ways. The ones who have evil in their hearts and control over their powers can inflict serious pain and suffering on the world. I am not saying that I believe you to be evil, Amon, that is not it at all. But you did come from a land that no one in this kingdom will trust. I need to you tell me, Amon, if you know anything about Jedah's plans for Aranyhon."

"I don't know anything," Amon answered shortly. His stomach turned over and wrenched. How could she not trust him? "If I meant harm, why would I tell you what I can and cannot do?"

"I don't believe you mean any harm, Amon. I'm just saying that some may think you do. I have to be able to assure them that you are trustworthy."

"Then tell them that I am not an Agorledian!" Amon said angrily, and he turned and left.

As the door slammed behind him, Veradella sank into her armchair. She didn't know who he was or what his purpose there was, but she knew that she could not lie to Aurora and Sadah about him. He was powerful, and now he was angry.

A black spider sat alert on Jedah's finger, and she held it up to her ear.

"Really?" she said deeply. "He has gained control? Well, thank you, my pet, you have done your job well." She sat the spider down on the table next to her. "Unfortunately, you are the barer of bad news." Her fist came down hard on the spider, "and I often kill the messenger."

Jedah flicked the corpse of the spider to the floor in front of Phober, who shuddered at the sight. Jedah rose from her throne and walked toward the large fire at the center of the hall. She placed her hand into the fire and pulled out a hot coal and began to fiddle with it as she paced.

"So the boy can control his Nexus, Phober," she began.

"If he has gained control, won't that make him almost unstoppable?" Phober tried to push the dead spider further away from him with his foot.

"Not necessarily, you fool. It means that this particular power will be strong, but he has little knowledge of other magic yet." She tossed the coal to Phober. The coal was cold, and Phober was examining it when Jedah, with a wave of her hand, set it ablaze again. Phober dropped it quickly and stomped it out.

Jedah went on, "I am not yet concerned with the boy. He could never overcome my strength. However, if he joins with Veradella's magic and Aurora and Sadah's brains, that is a concern. Aurora will be on guard against me. This is why we will not enter her kingdom until the perfect moment when she is at her weakest—after Agron has unwittingly provided a diversion for me."

She returned to her throne and allowed herself to sink deep into it. "Patience is a virtue that I do not possess. However, I will force myself to wait. In the meantime, I'll send some unpleasantness Aurora's was just so she does not feel neglected."

An ominous grin broke out on her face as she lifted her necklace from her chest. The center jewel was a large ruby. She ran her fingertips over it, and it turned black, then back to red.

"Now my loves, go pay our precious Aurora a visit. You know what to do. But remember that she is mine to deal with."

A billow of smoke streamed from the jewel and took three human forms in front of Jedah. One spoke, "As you wish, my lady."

Aurora went for a walk after breakfast to clear her mind. She wandered over to the side of the grounds that was not being infringed on by the dark clouds so that she might enjoy the remaining sunlight. There was a garden over there just beneath her chamber's balcony containing all the most beautiful flowers, surrounded by great alabaster pillars with golden orbs set on the top of them. They reflected the sunlight a million times over. Aurora always found peace there. It was far from the rest of the grounds and castle, and hardly anyone came there but her. She walked through the paths, listening only to the sound of her heels on the cobblestone and the waves of the ocean beyond the shores below. She breathed in the fragrance of the different flowers. Then a cold air moved through the garden. It wasn't a pleasantly cool sea breeze but rather a slow icy wind. Her skin began to grow cold, and she could feel her heart racing inside her chest. The air around her tightened, and Aurora detected a foul odor in the wind. She felt someone watching her, standing behind her. She turned, and there was no one. She felt something tug at her hair, and she whirled around again. Again, there was no one. She turned to return to the castle, quickening her pace, but then she saw them. Three large bats swooped down and into a line. She watched, horrified as they morphed into hideous human forms. They were women but were terribly gaunt. Their eyes were black with no distinction of a pupil or iris. They had gruesome faces with gray skin and sunken eyes. Black and stringy hair hung about their cheeks and they were clothed in tattered rags. Staggering like living corpses, they made their way toward her. Aurora's eyes widened in fear, and the first of the creatures smiled a terrible smile with fangs like that of a woodland beast. The three then glided toward Aurora, suffering no pull toward the earth's surface. They surrounded her. Aurora tried to dodge them, but they moved to block her every attempt. When the three were but a mere few feet from her they levitated, preparing for their attack. They lunged!

"Your Majesty!" yelled a voice from the entrance of the garden. Aurora looked. It was Amon. He was running toward her. He threw his arms out, and the three women froze in midair just inches from Aurora. She looked closely into the eyes of one of them, and then she saw a red jewel around its neck. It had an etching of a flame on it. After seeing it, Aurora ran from the site and Amon followed her. Once in the castle, she locked the door behind them. Aurora leaned against the wall, her head thrown back. Her skin was white and clammy. Amon watched her carefully, afraid to speak. She saw him staring at her and she cleared her throat.

"Thank you for your help, Amon," she said, her voice was soft and shaking.

"Are you all right, Your Majesty?"

Aurora nodded. "Yes, I will be fine. In the meantime, you had best be off. I am supposed to meet with Lady Veradella and Lady Sadah about the tournament. Not to worry, those creatures won't attack me in the castle. It is safeguarded against them."

"What were they, Your Majesty?" he asked. Amon looked out the window on the door to make sure the creatures were still frozen, but they weren't. They were gone!

"Never mind that now," said Aurora, seeing for herself that the three villains had vanished. "I'm sure in good time Veradella will teach you about them. Now off you go."

Amon sighed and walked away, but as he did so, he looked back at Aurora. She was more frightened than she would let on. Her skin was moist with sweat, and she was still breathing heavily, leaning against the wall. Reluctantly, he left.

Aurora finally caught her breath. She composed herself a bit and began to make her way to the throne room. She entered the room, and Sadah and Veradella were already there.

"Are you all right?" Sadah asked when she saw the state her friend was in.

"What happened?" asked Veradella.

Aurora sighed, "There were Azemon, three of them."

Sadah and Veradella moved swiftly to Aurora's side.

"How is that possible?" demanded Sadah. "Their kind was killed off long ago."

"Apparently not," replied Aurora. "Jedah must have found a way of summoning them back."

"Jedah? What does she have to do with this?" asked Sadah.

"They had her mark carved into jewels around their necks."

"Aurora," came Veradella in a shaken voice, "you could have been killed!"

"And I would have been," said Aurora, "If Amon had not turned up."

"Amon!" Veradella exclaimed, "How would he know how to stop them?"

"He clearly is more knowledgeable than you two think," said Sadah.

"No," replied Aurora, "He froze them long enough for me to get away. His presence clearly was not a factor they had considered."

"When did he learn chronoseizure?" cried Sadah. "I'd like to know how a boy can learn to freeze time that quickly!"

"He came to me and told me about it." Veradella sighed. "He has an unusual amount of control of it as well. That's why he was able to freeze them but not freeze you, Your Majesty. We can only assume chronoseizure will be his Nexus. He apparently did it the other day. He froze a vase that was falling but did not freeze Marvino who was there."

"So now Marvino knows about this?" exclaimed Sadah. "That's just what we need. A big blabber mouth telling everyone that there is another witch in this kingdom."

"Calm yourself, Sadah," said Aurora. She was now sitting stooped over on her throne. "Marvino serves a purpose too. He's never given us any reason not to trust him."

"Except that he doesn't know when to hold his tongue," retorted Sadah.

"Enough of this. We have more important matters to discuss," said Aurora. "The tournament, Veradella, how are the preparations coming?"

"Very well," answered Veradella. "I have made up the challenges. Now I just have to prepare the stadium that I will need for the event."

"Where will you be putting it?" asked Aurora.

"Beyond the village in the western field," said Veradella. "It will only be a temporary magical structure. As soon as the tournament is over, it will easily and quickly be removed, allowing the farmers to begin planting season on schedule."

"Very good," said Aurora. "I think that is all for now, ladies."

"With all due respect, Your Majesty, I think we should be discussing the Amon situation in more detail," said Sadah.

Aurora stared at her.

Sadah chose her words carefully, "There is something odd about that boy. I cannot decipher his character, which as you both know is . . . unusual for me. And we don't know that he will be able to control his power all the time. What about his emotions? If he is angered or frightened, he could cause serious damage."

"Sadah is right," said Veradella. "You know, Your Majesty, emotions are a vital part of magic. One's emotions can affect whether a witch becomes good or evil."

Aurora continued to stare at her friends. "I am well aware that wrongdoings can be produced by an emotion, my friends. I will speak with Amon myself about the matter, and then we will meet again to discuss this some more. For now, I would like to be given time to compose myself a bit more after that incident."

Sadah and Veradella nodded and left the throne room. Aurora returned to her quarters to change her dress as it was soaked with perspiration. She arranged her hair again and departed for Amon's quarters.

Amon sat quietly on the windowsill in his room, staring out at the black clouds swirling above Agorled. As the cloud grew, his stomach turned over again and again. No one would ever believe that he wasn't an Agorledian. He wasn't sure if he believed it himself. After all, how could he not be? He had been in Agorled for as long as he could remember. But he never belonged there. He didn't know why, but he had always felt that he didn't belong there. When Veradella found him and brought him to Aranyhon, he felt right for the first time ever. He never wanted to go back to the dark kingdom. He wouldn't go back. If Aurora banished him, he would travel west and pray that he could sneak through Morkslott undetected. He did not really desire to be there either. He felt that Aurora would want to send him away, especially after what had happened in the garden. Clearly, there was something that she did not care to share with him. Could Aurora ever trust him? What could he do to prove himself? She couldn't possibly send him away. But Veradella made it quite clear to him his presence was unwelcome. His magic was not able to be trusted. He threw his head back against the wall and rubbed his eyes. It was hopeless. There was no way to explain his power to anyone. There came a knock at the door.

Amon jumped and quickly called, "Who's there?"

"It's only me, Amon." It was the queen's voice. "I don't mean to intrude, but I would like a word with you."

Amon's heart rate shot up. This was it, she would send him away. For a moment he thought of saying that he felt deathly ill and wouldn't wish to give her his disease. But then he thought who was he to lie to a queen?

"Please, Your Majesty, come in," he sighed.

Aurora entered and saw Amon scrambling from the windowsill and to his feet.

"Well," she smiled, "Marvino gave you one of our finest rooms—very good."

Amon forced a smile. Aurora returned the smile and sat down on the windowsill, indicating that Amon should do the same. They sat in silence for a while. Aurora watched Amon out of the corner of her eye as he shifted his weight again and again. Amon tried to keep himself from looking unnerved, but finally had to speak.

"Your Majesty, I did not mean to cause any trouble."

"And what trouble do you think you have caused, Amon?" asked Aurora.

Amon looked down at his knees. He could feel Aurora's eyes on him and did not dare look up. "I know that Lady Sadah dislikes me. I know that you all think my magic is evil."

"Your magic is evil?" Aurora said. "Amon, magic is as good or evil as the person who conjures it. You saved my life today, and for that reason, it is difficult for me to believe that you are evil."

Amon took a deep breath for the first time since the incident in the garden. She wasn't going to send him away, and she believed him.

"However," began Aurora, "there are some things that you must realize. You have an unusual gift. Not only are you magical but you have strength as does your magic. It could easily be drawn to evil. Temptation to destroy is stronger than it is to save. Anger, fear, distrust—they're all easier to rely on. You must know that you are not all powerful until you can control yourself. Controlling your powers is secondary. Trust me, Amon. I know the trouble that can be caused by a simple misjudgment of a situation."

"I understand, Your Majesty, but how am I suppose to learn this control? And when will I know that I have it?"

Aurora smiled. "When you are able to solve problems without magic and when you realize when to use magic and when to use your wits. Then you will have gained control."

Amon laughed. "I have no wits that would measure up to my magic. I can guarantee that."

"Don't be so certain," Aurora said, "Wits are a strange thing. A person can spend a lifetime looking for them and have had them all along. Intelligence is really just a fancy word for using your instincts. Now knowledge, on the other hand, should be sought after. That is why you should continue your studies with Veradella. When you combine knowledge with your instincts, there will be no stopping you."

"If everyone is so afraid that I am evil, why tell me what I need to do to grow stronger?" asked Amon.

"Well," said Aurora with a smirk, "let's just say I have faith in you."

She rose from her seat and walked toward the door. Amon rose as well and walked with her.

"Your Majesty," he began, "I wonder if I might ask a favor."

"Certainly," Aurora replied.

Amon looked a bit uneasy. "I don't really know who I am. I don't know if I am an Agorledian or an Aranyhoner or something else. For once I'd just like to know, is that possible?"

"What you are is not as important as what you wish to be," answered Aurora. "But here's one way to know if you are of this land. Attempt to enter the tournament for the crown. Veradella's gates will allow no one but true Aranyhoners to enter."

"Oh I couldn't!" exclaimed Amon, "I could never be a king!"

Aurora's eyebrows rose, and she smiled. "Are you so certain that you can win the tournament? You just try your best, and leave the rest to fate."

With this she left and Amon felt a relaxing wave come over him. He laid himself down and felt sleep tug at him and finally gave in to its pull.

CHAPTER THREE

Amon's Tale

"WHAT IS IT that you think I can do, my lord?" Marvino asked innocently. "I really hold no position of esteem in Aranyhon."

"Yes," began Agron, "but you are the only one that is even willing to hear me out."

Agron bit his lip and paced while Marvino remained seated at a table of fine mahogany wood. The room had a burgundy décor with lush velvet upholstery on every inch of the furniture. Marvino thought that it must be Agron's private den. It seemed a good place to ponder whatever people in power ponder about.

"Do you understand what I am asking of you?" asked Agron, bending over the arm of Marvino's chair. Marvino was taken aback by the close proximity of Agron's face to his, so he shifted to the other side of the chair.

"Explain what you are asking of me again, my lord," said Marvino.

Agron leaned further over the arm of the chair causing Marvino to jump. Agron grew frenzied. "I need you to convince your queen that I mean no harm. I am only concerned for the well-being of Aranyhon. If it were to fall to Agorled, it would be disastrous! Not to mention that it is simply not fair to shut me out of Aranyhon. I'm not a criminal!"

"I understand," Marvino replied, trying to move further away from Agron, "but like I said, I don't know if my word alone will convince Queen Aurora that you are trying to help her. I can't imagine how you got wind of Jedah's plot before us. The rumors must have spread through our people without reaching the castle somehow."

"Well, the truth is," began Agron, trying to keep himself together, "well, no, I really shouldn't say."

"Yes, my lord, what is it?"

"Well, it's just that, I don't think Aurora's subjects are as loyal as they should be." Agron sighed so convincingly that Marvino's concern grew instantly.

"How can that be? Why?" he asked.

Agron leapt to his feet and began to pace again, "Marvino, have you heard of Lady Veradella?"

"Well, yes, of course!" Marvino smiled. "She is wonderful! She rarely even scolds me whenever she must repair a valuable I've broken."

Agron was face-to-face with Marvino again. "Marvino! Veradella is a dark witch! Don't you see it?"

Marvino jumped up. "Now see here, my lord, with all do respect, Lady Veradella is a sweet, dear lady whose magic is well received by all who truly know her! If you think that she would ever harm another you are mad!"

Agron's face flushed. "I'm not mad," he said flatly.

The two men stared into each other's eyes for a moment. Agron finally forced himself to move away from Marvino and began speaking frantically again.

"Marvino," he said, "I'm sure Veradella seems kind and harmless enough. But who can you really trust these days? Besides, you cannot tell me that nothing strange has been happening lately!"

Marvino sank into his seat again. "No," he whispered, "it can't be."

He was speaking more to himself than to Agron.

"What can't be?" probed Agron, his eyebrows rising.

"The boy," Marvino thought aloud.

"What boy? What are you talking about?" Agron asked. He had been thinking of the cloud when he spoke of strange occurrences.

"Veradella's apprentice," Marvino answered. "He stopped a falling vase in midair the other day right in front of my eyes. I've never seen anything like it. It was clearly unnatural, especially for a witch so young."

Marvino's face was drawn. Agron's face, however, was twitching in excitement. He had come across information he had not expected to find. Veradella had an apprentice, a boy who could freeze objects in motion. A chill ran down Marvino's spine has he watched Agron's face light up and his eyes flash.

"My lord?"

Agron snapped out of his trance. "Marvino," his voice growing more hysterical than ever, "this boy is a danger, just as Veradella is a danger. Something must be done!" He rose and began pacing once more, trying to control himself and maintaining his façade for Marvino. "Do you know what this means? Jedah has spies in Aranyhon! She can now attack from within as well as from without! And they say I'm dangerous! They say I'm crazy!"

"I've heard enough!" yelled Marvino rising from his seat again. "You are crazy! I can't believe I ever considered you to be an honest man. You would rather Aranyhon be weakened with distrust and disloyalty, but you will not succeed! My trust and loyalty lies with Her Majesty, Queen Aurora! You, my lord, are a coward and you have every right to be one! When I tell Her Majesty of your treachery she will come for you! Her will is stronger than your fortress walls!"

He turned and reached the door. He only saw a white light shoot toward him and then darkness.

"Well done, Rochero," said Agron. "He nearly got away from me."

"Are you all right, master?" Rochero emerged from the smoke, stepping over Marvino's motionless body.

"Certainly, I can take care of myself, Rochero," said Agron, harshly. "I'm not a child!"

"Yes master, but you must control yourself if you are to convince everyone that you are Marvino at that tournament," scolded Rochero.

Agron's eyes flashed. "Where do you get off telling me what to I should and should not do?" yelled Agron. "You are nothing, Rochero! Don't try controlling me, or you might find yourself with nowhere but Agorled to go! And Jedah would kill you just for the sport of it! I don't need you! I could be king without you, so just do your job!"

Rochero's expression was unshaken and as cold as a rock. "Very well, master. I shall tend to my duties and see that this scum finds his place in the dungeons to rot."

Weeks had gone by, and Aurora still had the same dream. Each night it grew clearer. She saw herself at six years old once again, and she realized she was in the dream. Her young self ran through the field of tall grass, but that dark figure still loomed on the hill watching her. Or was the figure staring at Aurora herself? Yes, it was not watching the child form of Aurora but was staring back at her grown self! The air around Aurora grew cold and then colder, but the young Aurora skipped through the grass still. Aurora wanted to awake. She shut her eyes tight but knew that she must face this dream, so she decided to watch on. She looked up, and the dark figure had disappeared from the hillside. Where had it gone? Aurora turned around, frantically searching for the dark hooded being. When she circled a third time, the field was gone, and she was now in a courtyard of stone. She turned around again and saw herself at ten years of age. But this Aurora was angry, not cheerful as the six-year-old had been. The ten-year-old sat on the edge of a fountain, knees pulled up to her chest and arms wrapped around them. A door behind her opened, and she turned to see the dark figure backing out the door away from a man who was yelling at it with his sword drawn. Aurora's father had never been angrier than he was at that figure. Aurora watched her young self grab her father's other arm and plead with him, but his sword remained pointed at the figure in black. It continued to back away and fell to the ground. Aurora's father released his arm from Aurora's grasp and swung his sword to strike the creature dead. But at that moment thick smoke rushed through the courtyard. Aurora lashed her arms about trying to see through the cloud of gray, but the more she flailed the more the smoke transformed from gray to red. Once the crimson fog consumed her, a cold wind blew it away to reveal what Aurora had been so afraid to see: her father dead. He lay on the ground, run through with his own sword. The ten-year-old Aurora stood frozen at his feet, simply staring at the lifeless mass that was her father. The child turned and looked at Aurora. Then there was a flash and she saw the hooded figured. Then another flash—Jedah! Aurora was awake. Her face was dripping with sweat. Her lungs ached as if a boulder had been dropped on her chest. As she fought to breath, she threw the covers off and went to the window. She looked down at the garden. The golden orbs glistened slightly in the moonlight. Jedah had managed to attack her in her dreams just as easily as she had sent the Azemon to attack her in the garden. She washed her face and put on a robe of blue silk. She left her room as if she were leaving her father's funeral once more: bewildered and shaken. Without giving it any thought, she made her way through the halls to a different wing of the castle. She climbed a wide staircase to an upper level of the wing and turned to walk down the dark hall. She had done this walk before and needed no light to find her way. Wandering in darkness, for there were no windows in this hall to let in the blue light of the moon, she breathed lightly as to not awaken the walls. In pitch darkness she stopped and extended hand to find the doorknob with ease. She entered the room, closing the door behind her. It was only now that she lit a candle and ventured further into the room. She came upon a fireplace where she also lit a small fire. She then went to an armchair that sat in front of the fireplace and allowed her eyes to drift up. The man in the painting stared back at her. Although his pose and attire were that of a king's, his eyes were gentle. A tear rolled down Aurora's cheek as she whispered.

"Why did you have to die?"

"You always have had a knack for holding everything inside," came a familiar voice from behind her.

"How did you know I would come here?" asked Aurora.

"Well," sighed the voice, "when we were younger, you loved to play hide-and-seek. The trouble was you hid in the same spot every time."

Aurora smiled. "At least I didn't always giggle when the seeker was getting close."

"We always liked to pretend we didn't know where the other one was. It was the least we could do. Humor each other. Yes, we both have had our share of pretending." The voice drew near.

Aurora stared into the fire and whispered, "What am I going to do, Sadah?"

Sadah's face finally came into the light. She too was dressed in her nightwear, and her mass of curls was no longer pulled back in a bun but allowed to fall freely to her shoulders. She spoke softly, "To begin with, now is not the time to pretend for my benefit. Tell me the truth, Aurora, the whole truth. What is it that is troubling you?"

Aurora looked into her friend's eyes. She felt as though telling Sadah of her dream would only create more problems. Why worry someone you love when there is nothing they can do?

Sadah sat up in her chair. "Aurora, don't try to protect *me* from the truth. You know I will discover it either way."

Aurora shot Sadah a look of frustration then replied, "It was a dream." Her voice was tired. "It was a dream about my father's death and about Jedah . . . nothing more, nothing less."

Sadah let out a long breath. Aurora knew she was choosing her words carefully before she spoke.

"Aurora," began Sadah, "it is time that you allowed yourself to move past your father's death. It was not your fault. Jedah deceived you as she has deceived us all at one point or another. What happened that day was not your intent, and intentions are what matter. Your intention that day was to save a person's life, not to destroy one."

"But I did destroy one," Aurora said weakly. "I destroyed my father's. I was so angry with him, Sadah, and I was wrong for being so. I couldn't say I was sorry. He died before I could say anything—before I even knew anything."

"Yes, you let Jedah get the best of you that day, but don't let her do it again. By giving up and losing hope, you're letting her win the war. Darkness can only spread if no one is willing to be the sole light. Once there is one light, others will follow."

"But what if they don't? Then I am left alone to fight all of her darkness? I cannot win this on my own."

Sadah came to her friend's side. "You are not alone. You have Veradella and me, and now Amon, who clearly you can trust."

"So sure of that now," said Aurora with a raised eyebrow. "What changed your mind?"

"I have my reasons for trusting him," said Sadah.

Aurora smiled but only for a moment. Then she began again, "If Jedah is going to attack me in this world and the dream world, there is no way for me to defeat her."

"Aurora, Jedah doesn't even know of the battle going on inside of you. She doesn't know that you were that child that lost her father. She thinks that you are just like everyone else, which gives you the upper ground."

"She's strong, Sadah." Aurora felt defeated.

"So are you." Sadah's voice was firm. "And a person's spirit matters more than a person's ability. You can defeat her. But you will have to be honest with yourself in order to do so. And if I know you—and I do—you'll hold off until the last possible moment, and then you will rise to face your enemies."

Aurora felt more tears building up. Sadah was her best friend, and she knew she was right. She held the tears back but only just barely as she nodded to Sadah and rose from the armchair. The two walked to the door.

"Quite frankly," came Sadah, "if Jedah knew half the person you are, she'd stay locked up in her castle, hoping that you don't try to conquer her." They laughed. "Now off to bed," Sadah ordered. "I'll see that the fire gets put out."

Aurora embraced Sadah and allowed only one tear to roll down her cheek, but she quickly wiped it away before releasing her embrace. She turned and disappeared into the darkness of the hall, feeling drowsy enough to fall into hopefully, a dreamless sleep, when she returned to her bed.

Sadah went back into the room and shut the door. She lifted the candle they had used to find their way to the door and turned around.

"Hello, Amon," she said.

There he was, shaking and terrified. His mind raced for an explanation.

"Hear anything of interest?" she asked, but strangely her voice was not mean spirited; no, it actually was a lighthearted tone.

"My lady," Amon began in a very small voice, "I was lost. I saw you walking in the hall, and I thought that perhaps your bed chambers were in the same hall as mine, so I followed you."

"And when I reached this dismally dark hallway you found it to be odd, did you not?" she was clearly not scolding him at all.

"Well, I . . ."

"Not to worry, Amon, I knew you were behind me."

Amon stopped stuttering and looked at her with a puzzled expression. She trusted him? He had heard her tell Aurora that she did. But why? Sadah had done nothing but accuse and distrust Amon since she met him, and now she led him into a secret conversation she undoubtedly knew was to occur? He looked up from his thoughts to see Sadah watching him with a slightly amused expression.

"How much of the conversation did you hear, Amon?" she asked.

Amon lowered his eyes. "All of it," he sighed.

Sadah smiled, "I appreciate your honesty. Remember the bit where I said that Queen Aurora now had you to rely on?"

Amon nodded.

"Well, it is true that when I first met you I did not trust you. I felt sure that you were not as innocent as you appeared. You have to understand, Amon, I have a knack, a gift, so to speak, of being able to detect things about people. But you were a mystery to me. Then you saved my best friend from a trio of Azemon. And then made a request of a queen—oh yes, I heard about the favor you asked. Her Majesty told me. It is I that have been given the task of finding out just what you are, Amon. So shall we begin?" She gestured for Amon to sit by the fire.

Amon slowly made his way to one of the chairs, still unsure if he was really talking to Sadah or some villain that had morphed into her form. Sadah relaxed into an armchair and looked at Amon.

She smiled. "Perhaps I should explain some things about myself to put your mind at ease?"

Amon was unsure whether he should demand an explanation or not. So he simply let a nervous smile escape and politely nodded.

"Very well then," Sadah began, "as Queen Aurora's royal advisor, it is my duty to play a certain role in her decision-making. She and I have always felt the best way to make a decision is to view all the possibilities in a situation. In your case, Her Majesty seemed to trust you right off, which you can imagine was a bit unsettling for me. It was an out-of-character move on her part. Be that as it may, I decided to make sure you knew I was watching you closely. You fell for my scheme and you believe I think you evil, which is what you told Queen Aurora."

Amon gave her a startled look.

"You might as well learn now, Amon, that women talk about everything. Point being I had made my point. You knew that I wanted to know the truth. But that's when you amazed me—you, even under the closest watch and judgment, performed a great act of selflessness. You didn't care what I thought. All you were concerned with was saving Her Majesty. Do you understand what I am saying, Amon?"

Amon started to nod but then stopped and sadly shook his head, "My lady, why are you concerned with me? I am a nobody."

"On the contrary, you are a very special person. To be given the gift of magic is rare, and you are even rarer. You are able to control your powers at such a young age and have an unusual Nexus to boot. You are most certainly somebody. Besides, with or without powers, everyone is somebody unless they chose to be nobody."

Amon took a moment to digest this information and then replied, "What is it I must do to discover what exactly I am?"

"Well, I have one complicated question for you, and I need you to tell me the truth. What is your story as you remember it?"

Amon paused. His story was not one he wished to tell Lady Sadah, particularly now that she did trust him. But then again, because she trusted him, he couldn't very well lie to her. He shuffled his feet, and he felt Sadah's eyes watching him. He had to tell her.

After a deep breath he began, "As far back as I can remember, I lived in the dungeons of Agorled. Jedah never hurt me but told me over and over that I would learn to respect her or she would see that I suffered. Every day she would come to my cell and tell me that I was worthless, but she would never do anything to me. She wouldn't even come near me. The head of her guard was a man called Phober. He was sort of a kind person, the only one, I dare say, in that entire kingdom. In fact, he was the only other person I ever saw. The other guards were goblins, orcs, trolls. But one day Phober was left to guard my cell, and he started talking to me. I actually asked him why she didn't just kill me, and he said that she wouldn't dare lose such a powerful weapon as me. It was that night that I realized what he meant. I had decided to attempt an escape. I picked the lock on my cell with a chicken bone from my meal while the guards were sleeping. I had just about pried the bar up on a window to the outside when they woke up. A guard grabbed me, and I threw my hands out, and they all froze. I didn't stop to study them but pulled myself out of the guard's arms and climbed out the window. I ran in one direction, not stopping for fear that they would pour out of the castle to hunt me down. I ran and ran until the trees turned from a dark, blackened color to a greener, fresher one. It was then that I met Veradella. She was walking through the forests, and she seemed to be such a kind person that I felt as though I could trust her. I told her that I was lost and she brought me to the castle. I stayed for a week with her in her tower before she informed me that she was a witch. Then she began to question me about any powers I might have. She asked me if I thought I could be a witch. I never told her about my incident in the dungeon, just that I thought maybe I could be a witch. I didn't mean any harm by it. She began to train me, and I began to feel as though I could perform my magic on command."

He looked up at Sadah. "That's all there really is to tell. I can't remember anything before the dungeon."

Sadah looked pensive, but there was no sign of anger or doubt in her eyes. "Very well, Amon, I again appreciate your honesty. I will have to think long and hard on your story, and I will try to help you find your identity, but it might take some time. In the meantime, the fire is almost out. I think it's time we both turn in."

Amon yawned as a sign of agreement, and they rose from their seats.

"Lady Sadah, what happened with Queen Aurora's father and Jedah?" As soon as he asked this, he realized that it was none of his business, and he looked away from Sadah as a sign of remorse.

Sadah remained kind but firm. "That is something that you will have to wait for Her Majesty to share with you, Amon. I have no right to tell you about her past without her consent."

"I'm sorry, my lady. It was wrong of me to ask," he said then and remained silent as they made their way to the door. His face grew pale, and Sadah knew he was worried.

"Not to worry, Amon. You will be fine tomorrow."

"My lady," said Amon with a smile, "if a person chooses to be a nobody, doesn't that mean that he *is* choosing to be a somebody? A somebody that is a nobody?"

Sadah's eyebrows went up, and she smiled. "See you will do just fine in the tournament, Amon."

"Why is that?"

"You think like Veradella."

As the midnight hour approached, there was still a strong orange glow from within the dark castle. Jedah was fuming from the Azemon's complete failure to even frighten Aurora. She sat high upon her dismal throne, her skin like ash and her eyes containing the only sign of life in her; those eyes that flashed with enragement at her creatures. The Azemon kept their heads bowed as she began to speak.

"Well my idiotic friends," she growled, "what exactly is your excuse for this act of ridiculousness? You cannot even carry out a simple task such as this?"

"My lady," the tallest Azemon hissed, "we were caught off-guard by the presence of a witch! Aurora escaped. But we will not fail you again."

"A boy?" Jedah's skin turned perhaps even whiter than usual. "It was a boy, wasn't it? A witch you say? Amon." Her voice grew raspy. "That fool will soon suffer my wrath along with the rest of Aranyhon! But why, my pets, did you not return here immediately? Did you think you could hide from me? Or perhaps you were thirsty? I only hope that your insolence has not given the surrounding kingdoms reason to believe that I am up to no good. Remember, I am your giver of life. Without me, there was no hope for your race. Do not disappoint me again. The only reason you are being spared now is that I will need you shortly. Do you understand me?"

"Yes, my lady," said the Azemon, her fangs slightly bared, "my apologies for our shortcomings."

"Go, and prepare all of the Azemon you have. I will need you all tomorrow, and you will find there will be a great deal of blood for you."

The Azemon snarled as a sign of pleasure. Their fangs glimmered in the firelight. Their eyes deepened, each into an abyss of blackness, as the mark on their jewels grew fiercely red, and Jedah let out a small ominous laugh.

Chapter Four

The Tournament

AMON BARELY SLEPT that night. His mind could not relax, and his thoughts were only on the tournament. Aurora believed he could compete but Amon did not. All the same, it was the only way he would ever know if evil lurked inside of him. He must at least try, but how dangerous would it be? Veradella surely would not make it deadly. Or would she? Once the morning light was upon his face, Amon forced his exhausted body to pull itself up from the bed. He washed and dressed then slowly made his way to the dining hall for breakfast. As he entered the room, he looked at the suit of armor to his right just inside the doorway.

I'm no knight. Who am I kidding? He thought to himself.

"Knights can actually be bumbling idiots," said Sadah, seating herself at the table. "Don't worry, Amon, you will do just fine today."

Veradella sat to Sadah's left and said, "Yes, Amon, and should you have a problem, I will be right there to get you out of harm's way."

"Harm?" gulped Amon. It was true. It was going to be dangerous. Veradella let out a little chuckle. "It won't be as bad as you think, and you've got a good head on your shoulders."

"Yes," he said, "and I'd like to keep it where it is!"

Aurora entered the room. She wore a gown of gold with an intricate pattern woven onto the trim. Amon's eyes followed the curling lines for a moment and found them to make the same shape over and over again. They were circles with lines through their centers. He felt sure he had seen that shape before.

"It is time we were leaving, "said Aurora. Her hair was pulled back from her face, much different from her usual flowing waves. Two guards came to meet Aurora to escort her to the field. They lead Aurora and her party to a tent adjacent to the stadium Veradella had created.

"Where is Marvino?" she asked one of them.

"He is waiting for you in your box, Your Majesty," he replied.

"Oh . . . very well," she answered, "let us proceed."

One of the guards opened the flap to the tent, and great cheers suddenly filled Amon's ears. There was the field, and in it were three sections of stands reaching high into the sky and forming a half-crescent around a flat open space of grass. The stands were draped with yellow banners, emblazoned with Aurora's sun crest.

The center of the sun crest! Amon thought to himself. *That is the symbol on Aurora's gown. What does it mean?*

Amon tried to keep the symbol in his mind so that he could ask Aurora about it later, but the accolades from the stands distracted him. The cheers continued as Aurora made her way toward her box, which was right at the center of the middle section of stands. Amon followed Aurora and Sadah to the box and watched with a smile as the two ladies greeted the people as if they were family members. Veradella walked on toward a large gate made of iron. Amon knew what it was at once.

The gate must be able to tell if I'm from Aranyhon, he thought.

He felt his chest tighten as he looked at it. It was the most sinister thing he had seen in this kingdom, with its sharp, pointed peak and gargoyle statues at each side. He turned away, unable to look at the dark gate and saw that they had reached the box. Aurora sat on a throne, very much like the one in the castle, and Sadah took a seat next to her. Amon saw Marvino seated on the other side of Aurora. He waved to him but Marvino did not wave back. Amon took the seat next to Sadah, and that's when he noticed. Aurora and Sadah looked stiff. They looked directly out toward the field. They were regal-looking, and Amon thought perhaps he should be the same. When he turned to face the field he could not help but let out a small gasp. The tournament field was underground! He could see through the surface. It was as though the ground was made of glass but was clearly not fragile as he saw Veradella walk right over the top of it. He saw the entrance to the course work its way underneath the surface, and then he could see four chambers. Much to Amon's surprise, the chambers appeared to be empty. *What must I do?* Questions raged through his mind as Aurora stood and made her way to the edge of the box, and the cheering resumed.

Aurora held her hands up, and the crowd grew silent. "My friends," she spoke with regalness and strength, "I have been proud to serve as your Queen. It has been my honor and privilege. You are a fine people. But my reign has now reached its end, and it is time to name my successor." The crowd cheered, and

Aurora held her hands up again. "Today, you shall witness history. Whoever I name the victor of this tournament shall be your new ruler."

The stands roared again and Aurora signaled Veradella to begin. Veradella threw her hands, into the air but the cheering continued. She waved her hands several times, but the crowd could not be calmed. The air was thick with excitement. Amon saw Veradella sigh. She then stood squarely and looked straight up. She flung herself into midair and remained there. Amon grinned. Veradella had spoken about levitation but had never shown him how it was done. The crowd let out another strong cheer and then fell silent. Veradella had the slightest look of bemusement on her face. Amon looked at Aurora and Sadah and was taken aback. They looked saddened by Veradella's display. But they then looked at each other, smiled, and returned their attention to Veradella.

"People of Aranyhon!" Veradella's voice rang out loud and clear. "This tournament represents all that is good in this kingdom! It is one that remains open to people of every status and will be won by the person who shows the qualities that we would desire in a leader: bravery, honesty, kindness, and wisdom." The crowd cheered, but Veradella was not finished. "Therefore," she began again with a louder voice, "the tournament shall be made up of four challenges that will test our participants. As you see, no one can view what is in store for our competitors. You only may see when a person moves to the next chamber. This is so no one will have an advantage. Should anyone need assistance in case of danger, I shall be at hand. Again, the competition is open to all that are true Aranyhoners and that are at least sixteen years of age. Anyone that does not meet these requirements will be *removed* from the field. With all that being said, anyone who is interested in competing for the throne, come down to the gate area, and let the tournament begin!"

The loudest cheers from crown were heard as Veradella lowered herself back to the ground and proceeded to the gate to meet the contenders for the crown. Amon felt as though he was glued to his chair. He could not bring himself to make his way to the field as others were doing. He tried to look to Aurora and Sadah without being obvious. They still sat rigid and serious, with their eyes fixed straight ahead. He thought they did not look like themselves at all. Just as Amon was about to ask if everything were all right, Marvino got to his feet.

"I think I shall try for this," he said in a low voice, "If you will excuse me, Your Majesty?"

Aurora looked to him with stern eyes and gave a small nod. With that Marvino began to descend from the box, biting his nails the whole way.

"What is it, Sadah?" Aurora spoke quickly, and Amon turned to listen.

"That's Agron. I can *feel* it," said Sadah quietly.

"Of course," said Aurora, "Marvino would never have met me in the box. He would have been at the castle to escort me himself."

"Exactly," said Sadah. "What should we do?"

Amon felt a strong feeling inside, one he could never describe to anyone. Every fiber of his being told him he must stop Agron. Without a word, he leapt to his feet and rushed after Agron.

"Amon, don't!" called Sadah.

Agron had reached the gate area and was mingling with the other competitors. Amon watched him push through the crowd toward the front, and without a second thought, Amon dove at Agron, pushing him to the ground. Agron attempted to get to his feet, but Amon beat him to it and grabbed him by the arm and thrust him to the ground. Agron rolled toward the gate, and as soon as he crossed the threshold, it happened. Veradella had said anyone that was ineligible would be removed. A blue gel-like shield formed within the archway and when Agron hit it, he was sent flying backward into the small group of competitors. Agron jumped to his feet and glared back at Amon. His disguise had been destroyed. He no longer appeared to be Marvino but was revealed. He came at Amon and pushed him toward the gate with such a force that Amon left the ground. Amon braced himself for impact with the blue wall but at the last second the gel turned into a yellow net. It caught him and gently placed him beyond the dark gate.

"You stupid brat," shouted Agron, and he began to make his way toward Amon again.

He only stopped when he saw the two gargoyles begin to bare their teeth and shed their stone bodies off to be replaced by living skin. Agron backed away not believing his eyes. The gargoyles leapt forward, blocking Agron's path toward the gate and Amon. Agron looked around in fear. As he backed away, Amon could see another man make his way through the crowd.

"My lord!" the man called, and Agron whirled and grabbed the arm of the man. The man reached in his pocket and threw a small gem to the ground which let out a puff of green smoke, and they were gone.

Veradella turned to look at Amon, who had a look of complete puzzlement on his face.

"Rochero," she said. "I knew he'd be here."

Amon began to walk toward her when suddenly, he saw the gargoyles walking toward him. Their teeth were still bared, and Amon froze not knowing what to do. He looked at Veradella. She was watching carefully, but did nothing. The gargoyles continued toward Amon. He did not back away. He didn't dare move. One gargoyle flanked him on his left, the other on his right, and as he prepared to freeze them if they were to strike, they sat on either side of him, looking up to Aurora. Amon's eyes shot to the queen as well. With the proudest of looks, Aurora rose to her feet, and the crowd's loud puzzlement grew silent.

"It seems that my gargoyles have deemed you fit for the tournament, young man." Her eyes twinkled. "Will you do us the honor of competing for the crown?"

Terrified, Amon glanced at the gargoyle on his right. Its gaze was now fixed upon him, but its eyes were gentle. It held an expression of anticipation, and Amon knew that, with the rest of the hushed crowd, it was awaiting his answer. He paused and his gaze returned to Aurora. Gathering all his courage he replied, "It would be my honor, Your Majesty."

The crowd cheered yet again, the gargoyles let out a roar in approval and returned to their posts and to their former state of stone. Veradella came to Amon's side and accompanied him to the gathering of contestants. A man with a small scar on his right cheek came forward. He was a middle-aged man who seemed worn and down-trodden. Amon could imagine he had fought a few battles in his life. The man turned to Amon. "You have a stronger heart than I." He turned to Veradella and smiled. "I withdraw." Two other men and one woman did the same. Veradella gathered the remaining contestants around her. There were five altogether. The two men to Veradella's right looked as though they were brothers. The younger of the two was pallid, his eyes wide open and fixed upon Veradella as she spoke. The older one held a small rock in his hand that he fidgeted with and eventually began to toss from hand to hand. The two women to Veradella's left were certainly not related. The first was tall and slender with chocolate brown hair cropped at her chin. Her eyes never stopped moving. They shot from one person to the next with a look of complete distrust. The second woman was shorter and stocky, and her long locks of hair were a deep auburn color. She was, Amon thought, extremely beautiful and delicate, but she asked the most questions. Questions that, Amon thought, were not of an advanced level. And finally there stood Amon, directly across from Veradella. She spoke at a quickened pace, explaining the fact that each chamber would test their skills and only when they passed the first chamber would they be allowed into the second and so on. After giving these final instructions, she had the five form themselves into a circle. She instructed them to hold out their right hand in a fist and tap the person's hand to their left with their left hand. They then were told to open their right fists, and in their own hands, they found slips of paper with numbers designating the order they would go into the chambers. Amon was almost relieved that he was last as he looked at his number five, but then he realized that meant he had to wait forever before he entered through the dark gate, past the gargoyles, and into who knows what.

The younger-looking brother was chosen to go first, and then it would be the older brother, then the redheaded woman, and then the tall slender woman. Amon hoped that the four would be eliminated or would make it through quickly. He didn't really care whether they succeeded or failed. He just wanted everything over quickly. Then he could get in, get out, and go back to his safe seat in the box. While all these thoughts raced through his mind, the first man made his way to the gate. Amon was sure the young man was shaking as he tiptoed past the stone gargoyles. The man came to the door to enter the chambers and looked back at his brother. His face was paler than it had been, and sweat was pouring down his forehead. His brother silently urged him on with a frustrated look, and the young man turned back to the door and vanished from sight. Veradella led the other contestants over to the side of the playing field. There they looked down into the chambers. It was the strangest thing. He could see the man through the transparent barrier along the surface of the ground. But the man was not moving, he remained standing there for a few minutes, and suddenly he vanished from the first chamber and reappeared in the second.

"You see," said Veradella to the four contestants at her side, "you will not be able to see anything that transpires in the chambers. You can only see which chamber the person is in at the time. It really isn't—wait. I'll be right back!" She shot her way onto the field, moving in a streak of light and arriving just above where the man was in the chamber. She reached her hand through the clear covering of the chamber and pulled the young man out by his shirt collar. He was in a terrible state, worse than he had been before. Veradella brought him back to the sidelines and as she sat him down, he passed out. She seemed to have little concern for the man's condition. The crowd was on its feet in amazement. Veradella looked him up and down then turned. "Next! You sir, I believe you are next."

The man looked at his unconscious brother, rolled his eyes, and headed for the gate. He did not waver as he marched into the chamber. Amon looked down into the chamber. In less than a minute the man had moved onto the second chamber. Amon wondered if this chamber would make him falter as it did his brother. But no, the man was in the third chamber in less than five minutes. The tension grew. Perhaps this man would fly through all four chambers without even breaking a sweat! As he watched and waited for the man to disappear and reappear in the final chamber, Amon realized that he actually was hoping the man wouldn't move on through the rest of the tournament. He wanted Veradella to be proud of him, and Sadah and Aurora. Yes, especially Aurora. She believed in him even when he did not believe in himself. He couldn't let her down. He had to be the best, not for himself but for everyone else. He stared at the man in the third chamber. He stared and stared. The man did not move on. Veradella seemed to become a bit anxious. The man had been in the third chamber for nearly an hour. Veradella moved onto the field not in a stream of light this time but in a slow walk, looking down at the man beneath her. Then it hit Amon; Veradella could see what everyone else couldn't. She could see what the man was doing, what was happening down in the chamber. She knelt down, her hand at the ready. All at once she thrust her hand through the barrier and yanked the man out of the chamber. He was covered in scorch marks, and dark hair sizzled at the ends where it seemed to have been on fire. The crowd gasped at his state. He removed his arm from Veradella's grasp and walked himself over to the sidelines.

"Next contender," Veradella called, as she followed the man to the side of the field. The redheaded woman studied the man as he got closer to the sideline. She looked a little concerned but walked off toward the gate. She entered and the crowd waited, and waited. Nothing happened. Even the terrified young man had figured this one out. Veradella's eyes seemed to glaze over in boredom as she watched the woman try to work through the chamber. Time seemed to slow down and the crowd grew restless. Some even started to jeer and hiss at the poor redheaded woman, and Amon wondered if she could hear their insults. After much time had passed, Veradella seemed to even have lost patience with the woman, and she stepped up into position to remove her. She stood quietly, almost as if waiting for a cue and then suddenly plunged her arm down, yanking the woman above ground. To Amon's surprise the woman was covered in claw marks. Something in the chamber must have lost patience with her as well.

As Veradella escorted the woman to the sideline, the woman leaned into Amon and said, "Careful with those bendiths." Her voice was small and high pitched. "They have a bit of a temper it seems."

Amon did not even bother to ponder what a bendith was. He would find out soon enough. Once Veradella gave him the signal, he would have to make his way into that underground arena, not knowing anything that lay ahead. He fidgeted with his hands, hoping beyond hope that his power to freeze would not fail him. There was one more contestant to go before him, and she did not seem shaken at all. In fact, she seemed almost certain that she had no worries in the world. The slender woman strutted off to enter the arena. Amon's eyes grew wide as she zoomed through the first three chambers. Yes, she had been held up slightly in the third chamber but not for an hour like the older brother who now sat scorched and sour on the bench watching the woman move on. She was in the fourth chamber and Amon felt sure she would make it out, and that would be the end of it. He most certainly would not make it through the chambers as quickly as she did. But then again, why not? He didn't know what lay ahead. Perhaps the tasks would come easily to him, as Sadah, Veradella, and Aurora have all seemed to think. The woman seemed to have come up against a difficult challenge in the fourth chamber as she remained there for what seemed to Amon an eternity. Veradella even sat down on the bench. It appeared as though even she was certain this woman would make it through this tournament without assistance. But then it happened. The woman's screams came ringing from underneath the ground. Veradella jumped to her feet and ran to the field. She did not merely plunge her arm into the ground to assist the woman. She dove completely through the ground to save her. The crowd was on its feet, and murmurs were traveling through the crowd. Everyone looked completely in the dark, and they were. No one knew what had happened except Veradella and that woman. Amon looked up to Aurora and Sadah, and even they looked concerned and bewildered. Veradella reappeared with the woman. She had the woman levitating, lying flat out on her back. Deep gashes could be seen in the woman's sides, legs, and arms. There was a beast in that chamber and it had nearly ripped the woman to shreds. How could Veradella have not seen this coming? How was Amon supposed to survive this tournament? He swallowed hard, and Veradella looked to him. He rose from his seat figuring he should get moving. Veradella shook her head, and Amon quickly sat back down. So apparently it was not his time just yet. Veradella tended to the woman, using magic to stop the wounds from bleeding and then sent her on her way with a group of healers for further treatment. Veradella made her way over to Amon and said quietly, "That last chamber will not be a problem for you. Trust me."

Amon sighed. He had no choice but to trust her. He would be fine. She would not let anything happen to him. Veradella gestured for him to go in. He made his way to the gate, looked up to Aurora once more and to Sadah who beamed back at him. He forced himself to look away and entered into the first chamber.

Amon cautiously stepped into the first chamber, ready to freeze anything that came lunging at him. But the room appeared virtually empty. Amon walked through the doorway. The rock wall of the chamber slammed shut behind him. He surveyed the room. It was basic stonewalls and flooring. He looked up and was surprised. He could not see outside as he knew the crowd could see in.

"Now I know how a goldfish feels," he thought.

He looked back at the room and three ceramic vases had appeared. He reluctantly moved toward them, not really desiring to know what was inside. But before he reached them, small hands with sharp claws rose up onto the rims. They were scrawny light tan hands that looked hundreds of years old. As the creatures pulled themselves out, Amon realized these must be bendiths.

They were only about two feet tall with pointy ears and bubble-like noses. Their beady dark eyes were set deep in their heads which were slightly deformed and had no hair except the tuffs that stuck out of their ears. They began to move toward Amon, and he noticed that their feet also had claws on each of their four toes. They moved, hunched, as if their bodies were too crippled to stand erect, but Amon did not underestimate them. The bendith on Amon's left signaled to the others to halt.

"Your challenge is to get out of this room. We each can give you but one clue. But if you are to take too long, we must remove you." It's voice was scratchy and low.

"Remove?" said Amon in disgust. "Don't you mean attack?"

The bendith grinned, its teeth slightly rotten and pointed, "Shall we begin?"

Amon nodded. He couldn't really bring himself to speak. The first bendith spoke again, "The one door will be a step back, but sometimes that's the best way." Amon thought, but he had no answer so he looked to the next bendith who said, "The one door is here and will be here." Storing this to his memory, Amon looked to the third bendith who leered, "The one door is simply that."

Amon was terrified. He hadn't a clue what they meant. He would end up another laughing stock of the tournament and come out all scrapped and scratched by the bendiths' claws. But he tried to funnel all of that out. He had to think. More importantly, he had to think like Veradella.

All right, he thought, *I can do this.* He thought through the clues again, and the bendiths flipped their vases over to sit on them as stools. They watched Amon with satisfied glares as he paced and thought. Amon felt sure they were practically dying to pounce on him but he tried to put them out of his mind, concentrating only on the clues. Veradella would put a simple answer into a complex issue. He thought harder and moved back to the place in the room where he first came in.

He thought, *the one door will be a step back.*

He took a step back. He turned to see where he had entered the room. *The one door is here AND will be here.*

"The 'one door'" he said aloud, "'is simply that'. It is simply one door, this door."

He looked over his shoulder at the bendiths. Was he right? He must be. They looked so surprised. He looked back at the wall where the door had been.

"Open," Amon said timidly.

The stones began to glow, and they traveled around the chamber. The shining stones formed a door on the opposite side of the room. Then that door opened. He had done it! He had made it through the first chamber. He was not completely unworthy of being in this tournament. His heart soared as he headed for the doorway, but then in a flash the bendiths were between him and the door.

"Have no fear," said the one bendith seeing Amon's alarm, "Yes, you have completed the first chamber. We are now to give you a clue to each of the challenges to come. My clue is 'a short-term answer comes with a long-term price.'" The second bendith approached him and spoke, "Remember, everyone serves a purpose." Finally the third spoke up, "Hear my words: 'Lies can be the undoing of even the greatest of things.'"

With this the bendiths slowly faded away and were gone, leaving the way to the second chamber open. Amon took in a breath and moved through the doorway. As he did this, he heard roars of applause from above him.

Never mind that, he thought, *keep your focus.*

The second chamber was carpeted in deep red and was lit by torches on the walls. The door slammed behind him, and Amon laughed at himself for jumping as he should have known that was coming. His eyes scanned the room before him. There were two doors across the way. One lay at the top of a pile of large rocks, nothing all that terrifying, though it would require a bit of climbing. The second door was not as easy a destination. As Amon drew nearer, the door's hazards appeared before him. From the floor rose stone-dragon-headed figures that began to throw fireballs across the path. Spears also popped up from the floor surrounding the path; there was no way to avoid the flame-throwing. He'd have to go through it. The first door was appealing but the bendith had given him an obvious clue.

A short-term answer comes with a long-term price, he reminded himself.

Amon watched the fire shooting from dragon to dragon, searching for a pattern. There was none. They were shooting at random. Amon attempted to freeze the flames but there was no such luck. Veradella must have planned for that, and Amon had just a twinge of resentment for her at the moment. But he understood the lesson here: magic cannot solve everything. Aurora had said he would know he gained control when he knew when to use magic and when not to. Clearly this was a time to rely on his mind. There had to be something he was missing. He began to watch the flames again. His eyes then wandered from the flames to the dragonheads, and that's when he saw it. When a flame was about to be thrown, the eyes of the dragon glowed red. That was the trick. There was about a foot between each line of fire so if he played it right he could slowly make his way to the door. Amon did not think about it anymore because he knew he would back down. When the eyes of the nearest dragon lit up he stepped back and once they were out he bolted for it, then stopped short. That wasn't so horrible. Then from the right, a blade swung down from the ceiling, which he ducked to avoid. It swung back, the second dragon's eyes glowed, there was a flame, the blade swung again, he ducked and ran through when the flame was out. Once through he looked for the next blade, which came from the left this time.

Veradella stood above the second chamber watching Amon's every move. Her brow was glistening with a bit of sweat.

"You've got it, Amon," she said quietly, "Just keep your focus."

Amon repeated his pattern six more times and felt the line of dragons and blades would never end. At one point he felt the heat of a flame that was just a hair too close to his legs. Sweat was pouring off him both from the heat and the strain. Once more he ran through and looked up for a blade but there wasn't one there, nor was there another dragon ready to shoot fire. He looked up in front of him and there was the door. He glanced around a bit to check for a catch in the situation, but there was nothing, just the door. Before he even stood up from his crouched position he said, "Open." The door unlatched and opened. He waited a moment to catch his breath then rose and passed through the door. He again heard cheers from the stands above and the slam of the door behind him, but at this point he was too tired to care. Crouching down to catch his breath, Amon tried to regain his focus. He wanted nothing more than to get out of there unharmed. He had been below ground for only a little more than a quarter of an hour but it seemed like an eternity had passed since he was in the sunlight. He raised his head to see what was before him and jumped back. There was a creature staring back at him.

"You okay?" it asked, it's voice was high in pitch but very sweet and gentle. "That must be a terrible task. The other two I've seen looked just as bad, if not worse, than you when they reached my chamber."

"I'm fine," Amon answered and straightened up, "uh . . . thank you."

"Well, all right then, let's start!" exclaimed the little creature. It began to giggle and bounce up and down. It was nothing more than a puffball of hair. Its body consisted only of its circular head. From there, it had short arms with hands containing three fingers but no claws. Also, from its head came legs about a foot long. Its arms and legs were covered in fuzzy short hair, but its head was a ball of long puffy hairs that shot straight out in all directions. To Amon's amazement, every time the creature bounced, its hairs would change color. It certainly was a happy little tyke, and it didn't seem much of a threat.

"Excuse me," he said and the creature stopped mid-cartwheel to stare at him with its beady eyes and a smile, "Pardon me for asking, but what exactly are you?"

The creature smiled and hopped to face him properly, "You are the first one that asked! No one knows what we are because we are all nearly gone now. I am a shillykork, and thank you for asking. I find it rude when people stare and don't have the courage to ask. It's either that or they just plain don't care."

"I'm sorry."

"Don't be, you actually asked!" The shillykork gave another smile. "Come, come, we should begin."

Amon looked beyond the shillykork into the room, and he saw that it was pitch dark apart from the small circle of light the two of them stood in.

"What must I do?" asked Amon.

"Here, I'll turn on the light," said the shillykork, and she snapped her fingers.

Amon grabbed hold of the wall to steady himself as the room was engulfed by an enormous wave of heat. Red-hot lava covered the floor. Protruding from it were various islands, each one a little bit different. The door to the final chamber lay across the fiery lake. Amon was still scanning the room when he felt the floor rumble beneath his feet. He grabbed the wall again and the shillykork did the same. The shaking lasted only for a moment, but Amon felt the platform move downward.

"What was that?" asked Amon.

"The platforms lower themselves further into the lava every minute you spend in the chamber."

"So what happens to you if I take to long?"

The shillykork looked bashfully to the floor, "Well," she said, "I was hoping you would take me across with you. The platform by the door leading out doesn't shift, so I'd be safe there."

"Can you make the jumps?" asked Amon.

"No," she said, "they're too far for me. You'd have to carry me."

Amon thought for a moment. It was not possible that Veradella would sacrifice the innocent little creature, but it made no difference. He couldn't leave her behind. He wouldn't.

"Well," he said, "if I put you on my back, can you put your arms around my neck and hold on tight?"

The shillykork beamed, "Sure I can! And I promise, I'll return the favor to you!"

Amon simply smiled. At that moment the platform began to lower again.

"We had better move," said Amon. "Climb aboard."

He squatted down and allowed the shillykork to climb on his back and lock her arms around his neck. Her long, soft hairs tickled the back of his neck, and she clung so tightly he felt a bit choked. Regardless, he got to his feet and used the wall to steady himself as he made his way to the edge of the platform.

"Be careful, now," said the shillykork. "See how this platform slides downward toward the lava before you make your jump to the next platform? It's a slippery slope, so, be ready to jump for it."

"Hold on," said Amon.

The shillykork was right. As soon as Amon placed his foot on the ramp he began to slide at an alarming rate toward the lava. There was no grip and nothing to grab onto. Amon tensed his body to remain on his feet, all the while keeping his eyes locked on the next platform. He gauged the distance and pushed off from the slope. He hit the platform hard and had to cling to it. It was a small and circular platform, and Amon had nearly overshot it. The shillykork was strangling him, but Amon said nothing. He waited only a moment and then climbed to his feet. Even if the shillykork would let go and get down for a moment, she couldn't. The platform was just big enough for a single person to stand on.

"You all right back there?" Amon asked.

She let out a nervous giggle. "Never better."

"Well, brace yourself. Here we go."

The next jump was a fair bit easier. It was just a short jump and to a platform just a bit wider than the one Amon had been on. But as soon as he landed, Amon had to squat to hold himself steady as the platforms began to lower a bit more into the lava. He could feel the shillykork shaking against his back.

"Everything is all right," he said and patted her on her leg that was wrapped tight around his torso. "The next jump is an easy one too."

"Just be careful of the spears," she squeaked.

Amon stood, "What spears?"

On cue, three spears thrust themselves up from the lava floor and then slowly began to retract themselves. Amon watched them carefully as they slowly lowered into the lava and then disappeared.

"What are you waiting for?" she said, tugging at his neck.

"How long do they stay down?"

The spears shot up again.

"Not long," she answered.

Amon ignored her comment and waited until the spears were just low enough for him to jump. The platform he landed on was the largest one yet. It had a staircase rising up toward the ceiling of the chamber. Once it reached its peak, the downward side was yet another slope. Amon could only assume it was as slick as the first one he encountered at the beginning of his challenge. He climbed the stairs and only when he reached the peak did he realize just how hard he was breathing. Sweat was running into his eyes.

"I'm going to set you down for just a moment," Amon told the shillykork.

"Noooo," she said and grasped him tightly.

"It's okay," he said. "It's just for a moment until I catch my breath. Then we'll move on."

She whimpered a little but released her grip on him and slid to the platform when Amon knelt down. They were high enough that the lava was a good distance below them, so Amon sat down, hanging his legs over the edge of the platform. He took deep breaths trying to slow his heartbeat. The shillykork practically curled up in a tight ball next to him, digging her fingers and toes into the platform. Her eyes shifted about the room. Amon took one long deep breath and then got to his feet.

"See?" he said. "As promised, only for a moment. Come on, we should keep moving."

The shillykork slowly tried to get to her feet. Amon reached out to help her. Before he could say a word, the platform began to shake. This platform shook much harder and longer than the others, and Amon fell to his knees to keep himself from falling over the edge. The shillykork was not so quick and teetered on the edge of the platform. Amon reached for her and grabbed her hand just as she lost her footing and fell from the platform. He held her tight as the platform made its small descent. She gazed up at him with fearful eyes that began to swell with tears.

"I've got you," Amon said.

When the platform stopped, Amon positioned himself to extend his other hand down to the shillykork.

"Reach for my other hand," he said. "I'll pull you up."

She did as she was told. Amon felt around with his feet for the other side of the platform. He locked his feet over the edge and began to pull her up to safety. When she reached the edge of the platform, she grabbed his shoulders with such force he nearly slipped off the edge himself. Just as he moved her to safety the platform began to shake again.

"Hold on to me!" he yelled. "We're going!"

She threw her arms around his neck, tucking herself, this time, against his chest. Amon took off down the slope toward the next platform. He could barely see beyond the shillykork's long hairs that were now streaming all around his face. He did his best to time his jump right, and they landed with a thud on the next platform.

"Are you all right?" Amon cried.

"Yes," the shillykork whispered, her eyes wide-open but without any more tears.

They looked at each other and then stood to see where they were in the chamber. Amon was relieved to see that the worst of the chamber seemed to be behind them. There were only a few small, steppingstone-sized platforms between them and the final platform with the door.

"We'd better keep going," Amon said. "I'd like this over with, wouldn't you?"

The shillykork nodded. Amon knelt beside her, and she climbed onto his back and wrapped her small arms around his neck once more. Amon hopped carefully between the steppingstones and onto the large, final platform. He squatted to let the shillykork down and then flopped down himself, leaning against the wall of the chamber.

"We did it," he said.

The shillykork looked less certain and kept her eyes facing out toward the lake of lava.

"You should stand up," she said quietly.

Amon was confused, but her somber tone moved him to his feet.

"Stay against the wall," she said.

Amon put his back against the wall. The shillykork walked to the edge of the platform, still staring out into the center of the chamber. Amon followed her gaze with his eyes and found that she was watching a ripple in the lava. The ripple was moving quickly and directly toward them. Amon didn't dare speak. They were not alone. He watched as the shillykork's hairs slowly began to change to a deep crimson color. The ripple charged them. A large monstrous snake reared up from the depths of the lava. His scales were black, and flames were pouring off of the monster. Its fangs were the length of the shillykork's entire body, but she stood still staring back at the creature. It hissed loudly, and Amon saw that its tongue was also ablaze. As the serpent cocked its head back to strike, the shillykork jumped high into the air and released a thunderous roar. Her hair stood on ends and shape-shifted into sharp skewers that she released toward the snake. Upon being struck by them, the serpent hissed again but dove back underneath the surface of the lava. Its wake retreated to the far corner of the chamber and then vanished from sight.

Amon stood there, his back against the wall, wonderstruck. The shillykork floated from midair back to the surface of the platform. Her hairs returned to their normal puffy, soft texture as well as to a robin's-egg blue color.

"Phew," she said, "that took a lot out of me."

"How did you do that?" asked Amon, kneeling down to see eye to eye with her. "What are shillykorks exactly?"

"We are one of the many varieties of faeriefolk, and as such, we have some pretty nifty powers," she said with a grin. "As to how I did that, I can't really say. But I did tell you that I would return you a favor, didn't I? Thank you for not leaving me behind."

"I couldn't," he said, "you would have been boiled alive."

"It was more than that, though," she said, her voice growing mature, "There was one other contender who bested this chamber. She helped me across the lava just as you did, but not for the reasons you did. There is a big difference between doing what you know you should and doing what you know is right.

She took me across because she knew she would lose the tournament if she didn't. You took me across because you cared."

Amon shook his head as if it would help him to better understand things. When he looked up again, the chamber had returned to the dark, cool state it had been when he entered. That's when he turned to find himself looking at the door to the final chamber. Amon stood in shock. He had reached the fourth chamber, the one that certainly was the most lethal. His mind flashed back to how that woman looked when Veradella pulled her from the chamber. Blood soaked, ripped, and sallow, the woman and had been driven to the edge of death. *Veradella said you would not have trouble here,* Amon reminded himself. What had Veradella said during her speech? *Four qualities,* he thought, *we're being tested for four qualities. Courage was one, but that was probably the lesson of the second task. And,* Amon smiled to himself, *kindness. Surely that is the lesson behind the shillykork.* Then he remembered that the bendiths had also given him clues. 'A short-term answer with a long-term prices'—the second task. 'Everyone serves a purpose'—the shillykork had saved his life from the lava serpent. *But that third bendith,* he thought.

"Lies can be the undoing of even the greatest things," Amon said aloud. Honesty! That was the fourth quality Veradella had spoke of. Even with his relief having sorted out all of this, Amon felt a sudden stab of nervousness as he stared at the entrance to the fourth chamber. He felt something by his side and jumped. It was the shillykork still smiling and looking up at him.

"You had better move on. I am supposed to attack you if you waste too much time. And I really don't want to."

"Why are you always warning me of what's next? Isn't that favoritism?"

She smiled. "Well, you *are* my favorite. You cared about what shillykorks are!"

Amon smiled. "Well then I guess here goes nothing." With this he moved through the door, which he knew would slam behind him. The final chamber was poorly lit, and Amon moved slowly so as to not trip. It was distinctly cold in the chamber, and Amon felt himself shiver. It had been so hot in the previous chamber, now the sweat upon his face was chilling him quickly. The chamber had a crushing pressure about it, and his shivers grew into a combination of the cold and fear. Then he heard something take in a deep breath. The breath was then followed by a voice.

"The final contender." This voice was gruff. "Perhaps you shall fare better than the other one I received in this chamber not long ago."

Amon plucked up his courage and said, "I wonder if I might see you. I feel very discourteous not addressing you properly."

The voice gave a small chuckle. "I'm not sure that seeing me would make you feel any more secure. But so be it."

Flames on torches lit along the walls to reveal an enormous griffin staring back at him. Amon was actually nose-to-nose with the creature, and he jumped back slightly. Manners, he reminded himself, perhaps they will help you again.

"Pardon me," he finally got out, "I did not realize you were there."

"Not to fret." The griffin's eyes narrowed. "So shall we begin?"

"May I ask what I am to do?"

"I will ask you three questions and you must answer them. No more, no less."

"Honestly," said Amon, "I must answer them honestly."

The griffin's eyes were piercing, "Is that so difficult?"

Amon thought for a moment. "Well, truth can be very different to two people," he finally said.

The griffin simpered. "That is very true. That is why I have been given the ability to see into your heart so that I may determine your true intentions. The other contender did not think to question me. You are wise beyond your years for doing so. Shall we begin?"

"Yes, I suppose we must," Amon said in a small voice.

"First question then," said the griffin, and Amon braced himself. "Are you frightened?"

"Yes," Amon answered without even a second thought. His answer just flew out. Amon gulped half in embarrassment and half in terror. He waited for the griffin's reply.

"As you should be," the creature said. "Second question, who should be the next ruler of Aranyhon?"

Amon thought. He did not want to say himself because he did not feel he deserved it. Who did deserve it? He didn't know but maybe the griffin would know whom he meant. He answered, "The next ruler should be the one who deserves it."

The griffin stared at him, and Amon began to tremble a bit.

"Well spoken," replied the griffin. "Here is my third and final question. There are many goods and evils in this world, and they both come in all shapes and sizes. Could you be evil?"

Amon could not breathe. This was the very question he had been wrestling with since he came to Aranyhon, and he was nowhere closer to the answer than he was when Veradella first found him. Aurora, Sadah, Veradella, and Marvino all seemed to believe he was not. But how do you know what you are when you don't even know who you are? How could he ever foresee what he could be without knowing what he has been? How could he know? He could be anything! His mind stopped racing. He thought again, he could be anything. That was it. But would that make a decent answer? The griffin had asked if he could be evil, not if he was. Amon gathered his strength and looked into the griffin's eyes. He answered, "Anyone could be anything, so I would suppose that yes, I could be evil."

The griffin did not smile, but glared at Amon with hard eyes. Amon felt him looking into his heart, and he felt so hopelessly vulnerable. Then the griffin stepped to his left and revealed the door that would lead Amon out. Amon's heart jumped up into his throat. It couldn't be, not him. He suddenly realized that Veradella would not be diving into the chamber to drag him out in the nick of time. No, Amon did not need saving. Somehow, he had made it through on his own. Made it through a tournament that he was not even sure he was worthy of competing in. There stood a griffin before him that deemed him worthy of the crown. And all of a sudden Amon became more afraid of walking through that door than he was of the griffin. If he walked through that door, he would be made king. *I'm sixteen,* he thought. *I can't be a king.* He stood where he was, frozen to the spot, dazed and uncertain. It was not until the griffin moved that Amon snapped back to reality.

"I thought your courage was tested earlier," said the griffin as he moved around Amon stopping behind him.

Amon turned to face him, "I can't do this. I can't be a king."

"Others believe you can. All that is left is for you to believe you can. You will not be alone. No one ever is, unless they make it so. And believe me, your strength of character will be known across the land." The griffin's voice, however deep and menacing, had taken on a fatherly tone. "Now go through that door, and take on your next challenge."

Amon knew the griffin was right. He could not hide from his fate, which clearly had been revealed. He turned and headed for the door.

Amon took in a deep breath and spoke clearly to the door, "Open."

The door obeyed and Amon forced himself to step through, and for the last time, he heard a door of that tournament slam behind him. He moved up the staircase, and the sunlight made his eyes squint. His ears were filled with the loudest cheer the crowd could muster. He immediately scanned the stands for Aurora's box, and there she was standing, applauding Amon with all the rest of her people. Sadah stood proudly next to her, and Veradella moved quickly to meet Amon with an enormous smile.

CHAPTER FIVE

Truths Revealed

"I KNEW YOU would do it, Amon. There was never a doubt in my mind. But oh, did you give me a fright in those two middle chambers!"

Amon laughed. "Well it's only fair! Your challenges gave me a fright several times!"

"And what do you think of our friend Alliari?" she asked.

Amon looked at her puzzled.

"The griffin," she said. "Alliari is King of the Griffins you know. You'd do well to befriend him. As king, it helps to have alliances with the griffins."

"I'll keep that in mind," Amon replied. His head was spinning. Alliances? King? Was it possible?

"Well, shall we?" asked Veradella, gesturing to him to present himself to Aurora.

Amon breathed in heavily and followed Veradella to the winner's platform, which was directly in front of Aurora's box and bordered with yellow and purple banners. Amon barely heard Veradella describing the difficulty of procuring the lava from the Volcano of Galgamon while he looked out over the hoard of people cheering for him, their new monarch. When he reached the winner's platform, Amon locked eyes with Aurora who gazed down proudly at him.

Aurora held her hands up to silence the crowd, "People of Aranyhon, I give you the winner and successor of the throne! Possessing the gifts of wisdom, courage, patience, and honesty, I proclaim Amon the rightful sovereign of this land. May the sun always shine brightly upon his reign!"

As the crowds cheered, Amon looked toward Sadah, but she was not smiling as she had been before. "Veradella, what's wrong with Sadah?"

After turning to face the same direction as Sadah, Veradella's face also dropped, "Amon, get Aurora back to the thrown room. Hurry!"

"But, what is it?"

"There's no time, Sadah has seen something. Something I cannot. Quickly, you must help Sadah protect Aurora. I will look after the people! GO!"

Amon raced toward the stairs to the box to find that Sadah had already urged Aurora down from the box, "Your Majesty," breathed Sadah, "Get back to the thrown room!"

"What has happened, Sadah? What's wrong?"

"Aurora, go now! They're coming!"

The sky had filled with a dark shadow in the west. Escaping from that shadow was a flock of creatures that Amon could not identify. Sadah pulled at Aurora's arm, but Aurora yanked it back and ran for her box once again. People had begun to scream and run, but Aurora's voice rang out over them, "Everyone, listen to me!" and they did. "Gather rice, beans, anything small you can easily throw into the air! I leave you in Veradella's command. Do not flee! Stand and fight, and we shall prevail!"

Aurora ran down from the box and people everywhere were running to their houses, returning with the supplies Aurora had ordered for.

"Azemon," she said, "thousands of them. Veradella! Look after the people!"

"I will! Aurora, get back to the castle!"

"Amon, come with Sadah and me."

"But what about—"

"Do as I say!"

"Amon," called Sadah over the crowd's yells, "Hurry! Jedah will be heading to the throne room!"

Hearing this, Amon raced after the two, running faster than he ever thought he could. He could not—no, he would not—let Jedah usurp Aranyhon. They reached the castle and Amon looked back across the field. There stood Veradella with crowds around her. Her staff was raised to the air. The thousands of Azemon were now clear as day. Amon could see their very eyes, black with all the hatred and anger of the world. They swooped down, and Veradella signaled the people. Everyone threw their supplies into the air and let them fall, scattering on the ground. In the blink of an eye, the Azemon's focus turned to the small objects about and began picking them up obsessively, one by one.

"Those small pieces will keep them busy!" cried Veradella. "Now everyone, go find sharp objects! We must sever their heads from their bodies!" The people once again ran to their homes grabbing shovels, axes, anything they could use to vanquish the Azemon.

"Amon!" shouted Sadah. "Come on! Veradella will be fine!"

"What has happened? The Azemon, they—"

"Never mind that now! To the throne room!"

Amon heard the screams of the Azemon as the people of Aranyhon wreaked havoc on them. Aurora, Sadah, and Amon bolted to the throne room's corridor. As they ran toward the throne room, Amon began to feel responsible for all of the danger that surrounded them. If he had not come to Aranyhon, Jedah would not be doing all of this.

"Amon," called Sadah, who was breathing heavily as they ran, "this is not your fault!"

He had no time to think of what she had said. As Aurora flung the doors to the room open, they all stopped short. There stood Jedah in front of Aurora's throne. Without warning, she threw a fireball at them. Amon moved to freeze it, but Sadah stopped him. The fireball was thrown back to Jedah, who, looking startled, extinguished it with icy wind. She stared long and hard at Aurora whose hand was held out. It was she that had sent it back to Jedah. Amon's eyes widened. Aurora let her hand fall back to her side and returned Jedah's stare.

"What is this?" came Jedah. "The young queen of Aranyhon is a witch? How could I not have seen this? It's not possible!"

Her frantic voice was answered by Aurora's, who said calmly, "It has come to this, Jedah. Too long have you haunted my dreams, and I could do nothing. Now we are here. It had to happen."

Jedah's eyes grew smug. "Zara—my, how you have grown."

"I am no longer Zara," Aurora's voice grew firm. "I have not been her since you killed my father. I took a name that would oppose you forever."

"And so you have," Jedah began to step down from the throne. "And let's see, I would imagine you have hidden behind this name until now in hopes of catching me off-guard. Well I am sorry to say that after two thousand years, nothing surprises me. And there is nothing I cannot do. I trust you know that."

"Pity that after two thousand years you are still stoppable. How degrading."

Amon just listened, absolutely stunned. Aurora could not possibly be strong enough to destroy Jedah on her own! Veradella did not even have that kind of power. She had caught up to them but watched the scene without a trace of surprise in her expression. Aurora was not a rash person. She must have a plan.

"There is nothing you can do, Aurora, I have taken Aranyhon. My Azemon will dissipate your kingdom, and it will fall into darkness just as Agorled did."

"You underestimate the power of the average mortal," said Aurora and indicated for Jedah to look out the window. Jedah saw her Azemon's weakness had been preyed upon.

"This is not possible!" screeched Jedah. "Azemon were wiped out! This generation knows nothing of them!"

"When you love your people they will trust in you. And believe me, Jedah, I have studied well. Well enough to know of the Azemon's obsession with counting. Well enough to know that they cannot help themselves when it comes to counting small scattered objects. And I think you will find that my people are strong-willed enough to stand up to the powers of darkness to save their home."

"Perhaps so," growled Jedah, "but now they will have no beloved queen or newly-appointed king to follow."

In the a blink of an eye Jedah was gone.

"Aurora," Sadah's voice was fearful.

Jedah reappeared next to Sadah, took hold of her, and disappeared with her. Amon gasped and moved forward to try to stop her, but there was nothing he could do.

Aurora stopped him, "Not to worry, Amon."

Jedah's voice moved around the room, "Is your friend a witch too, Aurora? Let's see how well she plays this game."

Aurora moved to the center of the room and paused. Veradella held Amon back. He watched as Aurora slowly turned around. She had her eyes closed, and after two turns, she stopped and opened her eyes.

"The problem with having a heart like ice, Jedah, is that incessant cold air that surrounds you." She gave a large wave of her hand, and Jedah appeared with Sadah flying backward through the air. Amon froze Sadah, and Aurora gently moved her back to the floor where Amon unfroze her. Meanwhile, Jedah was flung hard into a mirror that shattered upon impact. Aurora and Sadah moved to the throne, and Veradella firmly grabbed Amon by the shoulder and did the same. Aurora took hold of the sun on the throne and rotated it. There were three clicks and the throne opened a narrow chamber where two staffs were stashed. Aurora and Sadah snatched them up quickly. They and Veradella formed a circle and hit their staffs to the ground in unison. Jedah had gotten to her feet just in time to see it happen. The three witches flew into the air, spun, and returned to the ground. They were no longer in their beautiful ceremonial gowns but instead were dressed for battle. Veradella was in a blue skirt that flowed with her every movement, with a black shirt that was held taut around her body by a black leather belt. Her sapphire and brass staff shown stronger than it ever had before. Sadah was adorned with a long green collared coat over a black tunic. She wore rawhide breeches that were stained black, with thick-heeled ankle high boots. Sadah's staff was silver and had a bright emerald encased at its end. The handle appeared to be engraved to look like dragon scales, and she held it with pride. Finally, Aurora was clad in loose black trousers tucked into knee-high black boots. She wore a leather corset over a white blouse and gold bracers on her wrists. Her staff was a bright yellow gold with an amethyst stone. Its handle was bent into gentle curves that allowed her to spin it with ease. She wielded it more like a weapon than a magical instrument. And there among them stood Amon, staffless and feeling less intimidating than ever. He was among what seemed to be three of the most powerful witches in the world and was about to face off with the most evil sorceress there ever was and would ever be.

Jedah sized up her opposition with an angry gaze. Her staff raged with a red fiery light, its stone standing out so brightly from the ebony staff.

"Aurora, we must move quickly," said Sadah. "We're about to get more company."

But Jedah had already conjured up her power and soared into the air, saying

Aranyhon, here my call
From the skies your sun shall fall
From now on let darkness rule
While sunshine's trapped within my jewel!

The brightness of the sky outside began to fade, and an awesome white light flooded the room. Through squinted eyes, Amon saw the light funneling into the jewel of Jedah's staff. And then there was darkness. Veradella snapped her fingers, and candles around the room and in the chandelier lit. At that moment the doors to the hall flung open again, and there stood Agron and Rochero.

Agron stopped short. "Jedah! This kingdom shall be mine! I will not yield it to you!"

"It's too late, Agron," she returned. "Aranyhon is under my control!"

"Enough!" yelled Aurora and she flung her arms sending all three of the villains to the walls. "I am still the Queen of Aranyhon, and Amon will be my successor. Agron, Rochero, be gone, if only for your own good! You do not stand a chance in this fight. Jedah, I will destroy you. Not out of revenge as you would like, but out of necessity. This world is uncertain enough without you roaming about!"

Jedah maintained her glare, but Agron looked horrified. Turning to Rochero he whispered, "She . . . what . . . how . . . you fool! She's a witch!"

"Of course she's a witch! And you're the fool, not I!" shouted Rochero. "Do you know why you were made king of Morkslott? Because I made it so! I infected the king with his disease. I planted the idea in his head to name you his heir. And I am the one who has driven you to the very cusp of lunacy."

"I'm not mad!" yelled Agron.

"Yes! You are!" With this, Rochero whirled his cloak around his body. A silver flash sliced through the room. Aurora threw her hands out, deflecting the magic away from her and her friends. Jedah was not so quick and was thrown backward into the mirror once again, breaking the few remaining shards as she fell to the ground and there lay motionless. Agron was also sent flying and was now sprawled out on the floor, still as a corpse. Rochero moved toward the center of the room, his eyes wide and crazed.

"I'll handle this," Veradella moved past Amon. He had never seen her so determined. The concentration and focus on her face was an indication of her power. Amon looked at Aurora and Sadah for an explanation, but they both were surveying the situation in the room. Aurora's eyes were partially watching Veradella and partially glued to Jedah's body, waiting for the first sign of movement. Sadah glanced to check on Agron's state but then fixed her eyes on Veradella's position.

"She'll want to take him alone," whispered Aurora.

"She can't. We will have to intervene at some point," returned Sadah.

"What is going on?" Amon's voice was soft but steady. He had to know what was happening.

"Rochero was Veradella's magic tutor just as she is yours now. When his true colors were revealed she was very young, but even then she knew she would have to face him one day," explained Sadah.

"And of course it had to be today." Aurora's voice was tense.

"This won't take long," Sadah's voice had a tone of certainty. Perhaps it was that which caused Aurora to stop speaking, or perhaps it was that Rochero had begun to taunt Veradella.

"Well, do you think that the little I taught you will give you strength enough to fight me?"

"There is more to me than meets the eye," said Veradella, "and I've learned a great deal on my own."

"Well then." Rochero smiled an evil grin. A black mist, narrow but dense, soared toward Veradella, but she sent out a lavender light to meet it. Wielding her staff, she quickly shot another light at Rochero that took him by surprise, but he deflected it nonetheless. The fight raged with many more exchanges of magic. The two enemies had moved closer to attempt to hit the other with more force, but neither prevailed. Finally, Rochero landed a shot on Veradella, which sent her looping backward and to the floor. Rochero moved in to finish her off, but Veradella rolled and flipped herself back onto her feet just in time to parry his attack. She followed it up with a blow that then sent him flying back. He landed in a heap and did not stir. Veradella moved toward cautiously toward him to look for a sign of life. She turned to return to her friends when Rochero leapt to his feet with a newfound determination.

"Amon, quickly!" yelled Aurora.

Amon froze Veradella where she stood and Aurora flung her to safety just as Rochero moved to stab her with his athame. Sadah conjured a pair of throwing knives and flung them into Rochero's shoulders, causing him to fall again into a heap. Blood poured from his wounds, and he lay there stunned by the speed at which he had been attacked. Amon released Veradella from his magic and all of them moved in to view the dying Rochero.

Aurora was the first to speak, "Veradella, I believe a vanquishing spell is in order."

"I think I have one suited for this scum," replied Veradella.

> *Surface magic gives no fear,*
> *for magic within is magic dear.*
> *Without depth, power is lost,*
> *death to he who double-crossed.*

When she had finished these words, Rochero's eyes grew wide and fearful. He let out a scream that shook the walls of the castle as yellow flames burst out from within him, and he was reduced to dust.

Amon stood in shock at the power that had just been released from his tutor, but Aurora and Sadah seemed anything but surprised.

"One down," said Sadah as she turned to check on Agron. "He'll be out for a long time."

With that they all turned to Jedah's corner to find she was gone.

"Oh, not good," said Veradella.

"Not at all," came a voice from above them. Jedah ran across the ceiling and flew down upon them. One blue flash and Veradella was sent skidding to the wall as though her feet were pasted to the floor. Everything but her face remained motionless. Aurora held her staff in both hands, bowed her head, and thrust it to the floor. A translucent pink light formed an orb around the four friends.

"Go, Sadah! Help Veradella! I can hold her!" ordered Aurora.

Sadah and Amon ran to Veradella. Even using every hex and charm she knew, Sadah could not release Veradella's body lock.

"Amon," Veradella's voice was soft, "you need to concentrate. Sadah and Aurora cannot defeat Jedah on their own. Use your instincts and do not let her get the best of you. Remember, emotions can sway your thinking."

"I can't do this, Veradella!"

"You can, and you must."

Amon looked to Sadah for backup, but Sadah just simply nodded to him. He looked out to Aurora, her shield deflecting curses that Jedah was maniacally throwing her way. Aurora appeared to be in pain, struggling to maintain the shield. She could not hold on much longer.

He turned to Sadah and spoke, "We need a plan."

"Lucky for you I have one," she said.

After a quick explanation to Amon, Sadah went to Aurora's side and gave her instructions. "When I say so, release your shield and let Amon and I have a go at her. Back us up and protect Veradella. She's feeling a little vulnerable."

"Still making jokes at a time like this?" Aurora laughed. "Just say the word."

"Amon?" Sadah looked to see if he was in position. He nodded back in affirmation.

"I assume you have a plan?" Aurora asked quickly.

"Just follow our lead," said Sadah. "All right, after her next curse hits, release the shield."

Jedah's face was ridden with the most crazed look that her anger could conjure. With a huge gesture of her arms, she flung a curse toward the shield. Aurora's magic deflected it, and then she quickly let the shield disappear.

"Wait for it," said Sadah. Jedah seized the moment and released an enormous spell their way.

"Now!" yelled Sadah. Amon froze the spell.

"Aurora! Little help!" called Amon.

Aurora threw her hand out and sent the curse flying back to Jedah's unready arms. Jedah staggered backward a bit but managed to release another ball of magic at Sadah that knocked her off her feet.

"Sadah!" cried Amon. She did not respond.

Aurora came to Amon's side. "She's fine, keep your focus."

Jedah had taken a moment to relish in her skill.

"When she begins again, we will just keep up the fight as we did before. You freeze it and I'll throw it," Aurora whispered.

"And then she'll throw something at you, then what do I do?"

"Then you come up with a spell really quick."

"I don't know how to create spells!"

But there was no time to discuss it further, Jedah's attention had returned to the still-standing Aurora and Amon. The fury in Jedah's eyes emanated throughout the room. She threw a blaze of light their way. Amon froze it. Aurora sent it hurtling back to the dark sorceress, but once again Jedah sent off another jinx before the deflected one struck her. Her second jinx hit Aurora squarely in the chest and sent her straight to her back. Amon's mind raced. Veradella had mentioned spell work before but he had not studied it yet.

"Amon, breathe," said Veradella.

He did. With a deep breath, Amon closed his eyes and felt a strange warm feeling in his mind. Swirls of words formed in his inner eye, and he began to recite them as they appeared:

Evil witch with heart of stone,
Reduce to not but ash and bone.
Begone to hell and leave us be,
So long as the sun shines free.

Jedah had risen once more as Amon finished his spell, only in time to feel a warm sensation sweep over her. Her jewel began to shine a strong yellow color. All at once, the sun's rays burst from within her jewel and raced back to their place in the sky. Then a blaze of fire formed a circle around the sorceress. Jedah, frozen with true fear in her eyes, began to scream.

"No! It's not possible. No!"

It took just moments for her entire body to crumble into ash, her screams blanketed by the roar of the fire. The inferno extinguished itself and nothing remained of Jedah. In that moment, Veradella, Sadah, and Aurora all began to break free of the magic that had cursed them. Sadah rushed to aid Aurora in rising from the floor as Veradella flew to embrace Amon.

"That was some vanquishing! Better than mine was!"

"Well done, Amon," came Aurora. "I knew you could handle it."

"I don't know how I did it," said Amon. "It just came to me. The words, they just were there."

Sadah allowed a conservative smile to break across her face, "Yet another mysterious talent emerges. You can handle magic quite well."

"It was your plan," Amon blurted out. "I would never have thought of it."

"You'll learn." She smiled.

"Yes," said Veradella, "we will teach you."

Sadah's smile disappeared. "We?"

"Yes, well, you two are not in hiding anymore," said Veradella. "I see no reason why Amon shouldn't study with all of us. He should receive a well-rounded education. I can teach you levitation Amon, and, of course the basics of spell casting and potions. Aurora, she can teach you deflection and magical combat, provided that she isn't too rusty. And Sadah can—"

"Perhaps we should focus more on the present for the moment," said Sadah.

At that moment Marvino stormed into the hall. He was disheveled and tired, but he ran to Aurora, collapsing at her feet.

"Your Majesty, forgive me, I trusted him. I've been such a fool!"

Aurora replied, "It is all right, Marvino, there is no more threat upon us now. As for Agron, when he comes to, place him under arrest and find him a place in the dungeons where he belongs. His insanity was surely the work of Rochero, but I do not think it fit to release him into the world while the curse remains present in his mind. Then scour the land for Prince Arauck, the rightful heir to Morkslott's throne. He may want to reclaim his birthright."

"It shall be done, my lady."

"Now, I believe Aurora has an announcement to make, does she not?" said Sadah.

Aurora stood for a moment staring at the charred spot on the floor where Jedah and had taken her last breath. She stood silent as if in vigil, and then said, "An announcement. Yes, I believe I have a few to make."

CHAPTER SIX

The Death of a Father

THE DAYS THAT led up to Amon's coronation were cheerful and busy. Veradella oversaw the decorating of the castle, and much to her dismay, she had been assigned Marvino as an assistant. Her patience waned now and then, but he did his best not to make a mess of things. The occasional vase of flowers did meet its end, however. Sadah was preoccupied with the formalities of the event. She met with Amon once a day for several hours to explain the nature of being a king; everything from the boundaries of their kingdom, to royal appointments he would have to make the day of his coronation, to having him measured for his regal attire was taken care of during their sessions. Amon often left the room with his head spinning, but she was patient and kept the nature of their discussions lighthearted. Aurora gradually moved her personal belongings from the royal quarters to the guest quarters, but Amon had noticed that there was very little else that she was doing. She moved slowly through the halls of the castle and rarely spoke with enthusiasm.

The day before the coronation, Aurora went for a walk in the garden at the southern side of the castle. The sun glistened in the golden orbs, and all of the flowers were in bloom. Amon had caught sight of her from the window in the great hall. After his meeting with Sadah had ended, he made his way down to the garden as well, only to find Aurora sitting and staring across the ocean at the horizon. He quietly made his way to the bench.

"May I join you?" he asked.

Aurora smiled and nodded. Amon took a seat next to her and also looked to the horizon. After a few moments of silence, Aurora spoke.

"So tomorrow is the big day," she said.

"Yes." He smirked. "We shall see if I embarrass myself or not."

"Not to worry," she said. "Did you know I got sick before I walked into the throne room on the day of my coronation?"

Amon laughed. "No, no one told me that."

"Only because they knew I would never forgive them." She smiled. "Yes, I vomited in a pot of flowers just outside the entrance. That was when I made friends with Marvino. He cleaned it up without a word to anyone and took the time to privately check on me at the reception to make sure I was all right."

Amon smiled. "He is a good man."

"Absolutely, the very best. It's not really any of my business, but will he remain on your guard?"

"Truthfully, I have yet to choose my appointments. That is a goal for this evening before I go to bed."

"Saving it for the last minute? You and I are so alike." She smiled.

"I see no reason to not keep him. He served you with the utmost loyalty, and what are a few glasses and vases when you really think about it?"

They laughed, but Aurora's face grew serious quite quickly.

"You know, he worked for my father."

"Really?"

"Yes, Marvino was my father's page. He is the only other soul besides Veradella and Sadah who knew who I was all these years."

"Aurora," Amon began timidly, "what happened to your father?"

Her eyes went back to the horizon. A lump had formed in her throat as she began to speak.

"My father," she began, "was King of Agorled, before Jedah usurped his power."

"How did she do that?"

Amon saw that Aurora struggled to find words, but she remained composed.

"I suppose now would be as good a time as any to tell you my story."

"You don't have to if you don't want to. I don't want you to suffer if it makes you unhappy."

She chuckled. "Amon, it has been making me unhappy for a long time now. Perhaps it is time I talk about it."

She took a deep breath and turned to face him.

"My father was born into the royal family of Agorled. He had always known it was his fate to be a king and married my mother who was the daughter of a high official in my grandfather's court. From what I am told, they were very much in love and were seen as a promising pair of rulers. When my mother became pregnant with me, my father insisted that she receive the best care from the finest healers. However, she was suffering from many complications from carrying me, so my father turned to the magical world for assistance.

In his kingdom, there was a witch who had a reputation for nursing ailing mothers back to health while with child. He summoned her to the palace, and she began care on my mother. The healer was Jedah."

Aurora paused for a moment for a deep breath. Amon did not speak but continued to listen intently as she began again.

"It appeared to everyone that Jedah did everything she could to heal my mother's pain. My mother's health improved, and she remained quite happy for the remainder of her pregnancy. It was only a month before my birth that the trouble began again. Jedah put my mother on bedrest and remained with her constantly. She told my father that it was very important that my mother not be disturbed often and when she was, not for very long. For that entire month my father barely saw her. Jedah's plot was to keep him away while she placed my mother under a series of powerful spells and potions that would cause her to bare a magical child. You see, neither of my parents were witches."

"But why was it so important for you to be a witch?" Amon blurted out.

"Jedah wanted a young witch to raise as her apprentice. You see, in those days, Jedah had very little ambition. She wanted to have power, but she was content to raise an apprentice to do the legwork for gaining it. She made me what I am. She chose my Nexus. Deflection is a power that Jedah does not possess nor has ever been able to master. She chose my jewel. Amethyst is very rare in this world and possesses many unique magical abilities. I suspect Veradella will teach you gemology in the near future. I would not have been a witch if it weren't for Jedah and I am grateful for my powers, but it came at a horrible price. Witches are not meant to be created. They are meant to be born. She put my mother through such torment and pain that I only learned of when I traveled to the realm of the faeriefolk and read the archives of magic. There I read of how witches can be created and what the process does to the mother. This was years after I had left Agorled and Jedah took over. My mother died in childbirth, and I was raised by my father and Jedah."

"Jedah?" gasped Amon.

"Yes. My father had decided to keep Jedah on as a member of his court as payment for her efforts to save my mother. If he had only known . . ."

Her voice trailed off. She held back tears and went on.

"Because of her involvement with me since I was in the womb, my father never thought it strange that Jedah took such an interest in me. She and I spent a great deal of time together, and I thought very highly of her. She was my mother figure. It was when I was six that she began my training. She told me that anyone could do magic if they had enough desire to do so, and I believed her. She taught me how to control my magic and taught me the basics of potion-making and combat. This went on for four years before my father discovered the truth. Now, my father had always had friendly connections with the magical world. One of his dearest friends, Reichhold, is the chief of the vampire slayers. They are a race that was born out of vampires but are more human than monster."

"And the vampires are a relation of the Azemon aren't they? That's why you knew the Azemon's weakness," said Amon.

"I spent a good deal of time with Reichhold's children, so, yes, you could say I'm well-schooled in the history and nature of vampires."

"So, what did he do—your father? When he found out about your magic?"

"Well, he knew what my having magical powers meant, and he told me I was never to see Jedah again. That very same day, he confronted Jedah and had every intention of putting her to death before the eyes of the court for what she had done to my mother. He had no idea of the extent of Jedah's power though or her influence over me. As he moved to strike her down, I stopped him. I yelled for him to stop, grabbed his arm, and distracted him. Before I knew what had happened Jedah had used her magic to run him through with his own sword, and then she disappeared."

Aurora's strength finally had diminished and she quietly began to cry. Amon said nothing. He tried to take in the story in its entirety. It had been an unimaginable loss that Aurora had received, and she had held her pain silently all of these years. Finally, Amon spoke.

"Sadah knows of this, does she not? Does Veradella?"

Aurora replied, "Yes. They have been my best friends. Their stories are also somewhat tragic, but I am not at liberty—"

"—to tell me their history without their consent," Amon finished. "That is what Sadah had said to me when I asked her about your story."

She smiled, "There are some things that a person may want to keep for themselves. You know that as well as anyone."

Amon nodded.

"How did Jedah come to rule Agorled?"

Aurora rolled her eyes. "Oh, after my father's death, I felt so guilty that I fled from there. Without a direct heir to take the throne, the squabbling began and naturally Jedah was able to return and squash the competition. I practically handed the throne to her because I was too ashamed to do anything else. I fled to the forests beyond Morkslott, and that's where I met Sadah and eventually Veradella."

"And years later you competed for the throne of Aranyhon? Why?"

She sighed. "I made a promise to myself awhile ago that I would avenge my parents and destroy Jedah. After she lost my loyalty, she decided that she would conquer the world for herself. She became even crueler and less human every day. I vowed she would never destroy another person's life as she had mine. That is why I competed for Aranyhon's throne. Little did I know that I would gain another friend along the way."

She smiled at him. Amon returned the smile.

"But now that it is all over," she said, "I don't know what I will do with myself. Jedah is dead. That was my life's goal."

Amon felt uneasy. It had been him that had finished Jedah off. He possibly had taken away the very thing that Aurora had been promising herself to do. He now felt he had wronged Aurora somehow.

"Do not fret, Amon," she said, "I will never hold it against you that you, instead of me, vanquished Jedah."

"All right, how do you and Sadah do that?"

She raised an eyebrow. "Do what?"

"Read my mind?"

Aurora laughed. "Well, since telepathy is Sadah's Nexus, all three of us have mastered it. We have spent these past ten years teaching each other our own powers."

Amon's eyes widened. "That's her Nexus? She didn't tell me that! Why wouldn't she tell me that?"

Aurora's face grew grim. "I did not realize . . . Amon, if she had not told you about her power I should not have told you. You must not approach her about it. Sadah is very particular about the use of her magic and would not appreciate questioning from you."

"All right, I won't ask her about it," he said, "but I'd still like to know why she did not tell me."

"Sadah always has her reasons for what she does," replied Aurora.

Amon nodded.

"So," he said, "now knowing your whole story, I think I may have decided on some appointments to make tomorrow."

"Really? And what might those be?" she asked.

Amon smirked, "It is the king's prerogative to keep his appointments to himself until the day of his coronation. You will simply have to wait like everyone else."

Aurora glared mockingly at him. "Careful, Your Majesty. I'm still a stronger witch than you."

They laughed and watched as the sun slowly set on the horizon.

CHAPTER SEVEN

The Coronation

AMON ROSE EARLY the next day to watch the sun rise from the eastern terrace. He thought about everything that had happened in the past few weeks. He had gone from a meek young boy to ruler of a massive kingdom. His mind stretched to absorb the events. He watched until the sun was above the horizon, and then he went to his dressing chamber. Marvino had laid out his coronation attire the night before, but Amon had not yet seen it. Once he was dressed and while viewing himself in the mirror, Amon felt a chill run down his spine. The dark blue uniform was trimmed with golden thread and had a white sash that ran from his left shoulder down around to the right side of his waist. There were tall black riding boots to match the black belt. Spit-polished and shinning—Amon could practically see his reflection in the leather. Once dressed, he barely recognized himself. There came a quiet knock at the door.

"Come in," he said.

Aurora entered. She smiled as he turned to face her.

"Are you ready?"

"If I can learn to move in these clothes, then yes," he replied.

When they neared the doors to the great hall, Aurora put her hand on Amon's shoulder.

"Just remember," she said, "you earned this right. You and you alone must be convinced of your worthiness."

Amon nodded. He concentrated on appearing calm but felt his stomach churn with anxiety. Aurora gave a nod to the guards at the doors and they opened them quickly. Amon felt a knot form in his chest and felt like his heart was about to stop as he looked into the hall. It was filled with people from the kingdom, and they all rose from their seats for his entrance. Aurora looked straight ahead and Amon did his best to mirror her. At the front of the hall sat the throne as it always had. To its left was Sadah and she held the sword that would become Amon's. The blade was steel and had been forged by an experienced hand. The guard was gold and intricately patterned, and the pommel encased a plain stone from the courtyard. Sadah had explained to him that Veradella had cast a spell over the stone so it would take the form of his gem of power once he was crowned king. He was eager to see what it would be. Veradella, who was to the right of the throne, had the royal cape draped over her arm. She grinned at Amon when their eyes locked. Out of the corner of his eye, he saw Marvino step behind Aurora to follow her, as he was still her head guard. He forced himself to concentrate on what had been explained to him the day before during rehearsal. When he reached the step in front of the throne, he turned to face Aurora. As she turned to face him, she winked at him and smiled. He felt the knot in his chest loosen a bit.

Aurora began to speak, "By the law of the Kingdom of Aranyhon, it is demanded that no ruler shall reign for longer than six years. It has been six years that I have served as Aranyhon's queen, and I now must appoint my successor. By virtue of your integrity, wisdom, and courage, I proclaim you, Amon, to be the next ruler of Aranyhon."

Aurora turned to Marvino, who passed to her the crown of the kingdom. The crown was a simple silver headpiece with emerald stones. It was not an overly majestic crown, but it embodied power and wisdom. Aurora held it up before Amon.

"And so, by my last proclamation as Aranyhon's queen and by all the witnesses here today, I name you, Amon the True, King of Aranyhon."

Aurora lowered the crown to Amon's head. Amon heard a surge of applause ring through the hall as the crown met his head. His eyes met Aurora's as Sadah attached his sword to his hip and Veradella placed the cape on his shoulders. Aurora's eyes glowed with pride as Amon turned to face his people. When he looked at his reflection in the back mirror the plain stone on his sword had transformed into a clear diamond. A diamond—that was the stone that would be his gem of power. It had chosen him at that moment. Pride filled him for the first time in his life, and Amon felt a smile creep onto his face. But the applause died away, and he felt the knot return to his chest as he watched Aurora, Sadah, Veradella, and Marvino all retreat to the front row seats that were designated to them. He stood before his people now, alone. It was time to make his appointments.

"People of Aranyhon, I am truly honored to stand here as your king. Before today, I never thought of myself as royalty but simply as a subject of Aranyhon.

And now today and until my term has expired, I will continue to think that way. I promise to serve you, as a king should. I promise to listen to you and care for your well-being. And if, perhaps, I am less than worthy of this position, I will forever strive to be deserving of your love."

Applause broke out, and Amon heaved a sigh of relief. He glanced at Aurora, Sadah, and Veradella. They beamed at him. The applause subsided.

"And now, by the law of Aranyhon, I must, on this day, make some appointments to my court. These appointments are my royal advisor and my head of guard. I am also granted the right to form any other appointments I see necessary. At this time, I feel it is necessary to have an ambassador chosen to maintain our ties with the new monarch of Morkslott, King Arauck. In addition, I will place a governor in Agorled to oversee those far corners of our now expanded kingdom."

Amon paused and turned to look his friends in the eye, "And now to begin. Lady Sadah, please join me."

Sadah's smile was wide as she made her way to Amon's side. They faced one another.

"Do you, upon this day, accept your appointment as my royal advisor?"

Sadah felt tears form in her eyes. "I do, Your Majesty."

She bowed deeply and stepped to the side.

"Marvino," said Amon, "please approach."

Marvino hurried to his feet with some surprise.

"Do you, upon this day, accept your appointment as my head of guard?"

"I do, Your Majesty."

He bowed and stepped aside.

"Lady Veradella, please come forward."

Veradella did as she was asked.

"Do you, upon this day, accept your appointment as Ambassador to Morkslott?"

Her mouth dropped open. She was a bit in shock. "I do, Your Majesty."

She joined Sadah and Marvino on the sidelines.

"Finally, will Lady Aurora please step forward."

Aurora's eyes were already streaming with tears as she approached.

"Do you, upon this day, accept your appointment as Governor of Agorled?"

She struggled to whisper, "I do, Your Majesty."

Just barely clinging to decorum, Aurora bowed and backed away to the side where she was embraced by Sadah. Amon turned to the people once more.

"Do you, people of Aranyhon, accept these appointments I have made without reservation?"

"We do," the people answered.

"Then let them be so."

Amon bowed to his people, and cheers broke out once more. Amon turned to face his friends and was met by Aurora's open arms. They hugged tightly for what seemed like ages.

"Thank you," she whispered.

Amon smiled. "Just see to it that Agorled is returned to its rightful state."

"I will. I promise."

Sadah and Veradella also joined the embrace for a moment, and Marvino made a point of saluting Amon and asking for instructions. They then made their way to the reception in the courtyard. Everything seemed a blur for Amon. He watched as the people of Aranyhon danced, ate, and drank merrily. It was not until he noticed the gates of the courtyard being opened quickly by the guards that Amon came out of his cheerful daze. Aurora and the others were already on their feet by the time Amon knew what was happening. The crowd fell quiet as a man ran through the gates and flung himself to his knees before Amon.

"My lord and king, I had been assigned to a position of watch at the trading post of Belshire by Lady Aurora during her reign. I fear my news may dampen the spirit of the occasion, but I must speak."

"Go on," said Amon.

Amon's concern was great. The man before him had dried blood upon his face from a wound on his left cheek, and his clothes were shredded in places, as if he had wrestled with a pair of unfriendly claws.

"Your Majesty, there is something in the forest to the north. Several men ventured into those woods to hunt. When they did not return for weeks, I felt something was wrong. My suspicions were confirmed today when one of the men finally appeared. His eyes were wide with fear, but he would only speak gibberish. When I tried to restrain him, the man attacked me. We fought, and then he collapsed in weariness. After he woke he did not speak, and while he suffered from no visible injury, he died right before my eyes with an expression of terror on his face. Your Majesty, there is great evil there, and I fear it will spread."

"Did he cause you this injury?" asked Amon, as he referred to the gash on the man's face.

"During our fight, he bit me," answered the man.

Murmurs of fear and apprehension began to form in the crowd. Somewhere, Amon felt sure he heard a baby cry. He stood frozen, unsure of what to do. Sadah quickly came to his aid.

"Do not act at this moment," she whispered. "Be decisive but not specific."

Amon gave a small nod.

"I thank you for your haste, and I assure this matter will become my priority. It will be handled swiftly. For now, take your leave to the castle and rest."

The man bowed his head and made his way to the castle. Amon looked out over the crowd.

"Let us not concern ourselves with this matter now," he said. "This is a happy day."

The musicians struck up the music again, and the festivities continued.

"Aurora," said Amon.

"Once I establish a presence at Agorled, I will send replacement watchmen to Belshire. I will also send a scout team into the forest to see what is lurking there."

"Tell them to be on their guard. Did you see the fear in that man's eyes?"

Veradella spoke up, "It was probably not nearly as much fear as the man who emerged from the forest was experiencing. It sounds as though he was frightened to death."

"Literally," said Sadah, gravely, "but let's not assume the worst. And let's not think on it today anymore. As Amon said, this is a happy day."

"Yes," said Amon, "so eat up before your meals get cold. Excuse me for just a minute."

Amon rose from his seat and went into the castle. Quickly he climbed the stairs to the terrace facing Agorled. He wanted to take a look at the forest. He stayed close to the door so that the ladies would not see where he had gone. But even from the safety of Aranyhon, Amon knew it was just as he had feared. Whatever had driven that hunter mad and whatever evil the watchmen spoke of was a magical being. Amon gazed at the forest and the small black cloud that was whirling just above the treetops. It was dark magic, the kind that Jedah had practiced. He stared for a moment and then began his way back to the courtyard. He would celebrate his coronation today and worry about the cloud tomorrow.